THE
DOORMAN'S
REPOSE

THE
DOORMAN'S
REPOSE

WRITTEN AND ILLUSTRATED BY

CHRIS RASCHKA

THE NEW YORK REVIEW CHILDREN'S COLLECTION

NEW YORK

THIS IS A NEW YORK REVIEW BOOK
PUBLISHED BY THE NEW YORK REVIEW OF BOOKS
435 Hudson Street, New York, NY 10014
www.nyrb.com

Library of Congress Cataloging-in-Publication Data
Names: Raschka, Christopher, author.
Title: The doorman's repose / by Chris Raschka.
Description: New York : New York Review Books, [2017] | Series: New York
  Review Books children's collection | Summary: "Some of us look up at those
  craggy, mysterious apartment buildings found in the posher parts of New
  York City and wonder what goes on inside. The Doorman's Repose collects ten
  stories of the doings of 777 Garden Avenue, one of the craggiest"—Provided
  by publisher.
Identifiers: LCCN 2016026843 (print) | LCCN 2016046294 (ebook) | ISBN
  9781681371009 (hardback) | ISBN 9781681371016 (epub)
Subjects: LCSH: Children's stories, American. | CYAC: Apartment houses—
  Fiction. | New York (N.Y.)—Fiction. | Humorous stories. | Short stories. |
  BISAC: JUVENILE FICTION / Lifestyles / City & Town Life. | JUVENILE
  FICTION / Humorous Stories. | JUVENILE FICTION / Readers / Chapter
  Books.
Classification: LCC PZ7.R1814 Dr 2017 (print) | LCC PZ7.R1814 (ebook) | DDC
  [Fic]—dc23
LC record available at https://lccn.loc.gov/2016026843

ISBN 978-1-68137-100-9
Available as an electronic book; ISBN 978-1-68137-101-6

Cover design by Louise Fili, Ltd.
Cover illustration by Chris Raschka

Printed in the United States of America on acid-free paper.
10 9 8 7 6 5 4 3 2 1

CONTENTS

For Lydie

THE DOORMAN

ON HIS first day as the new doorman at 777 Garden Avenue, Mr. Bunchley was a little nervous. Mr. Hargreave, the doorman who had just retired, had been at the building— one of those grand apartment houses that make the Upper East Side of Manhattan the kind of spiffy neighborhood it is— longer than even its oldest resident could remember. Mr. Bunchley, accordingly, had a lot to live up to.

The duties of a doorman are various.

A good doorman must be able to open doors, of course. Opening doors is an art that Mr. Bunchley had studied and knew well. Not too fast, not too slow, not too wide, not too narrow, not too early, and not too late. Just so. Just so each resident of 777 Garden Avenue could enter like a queen and exit like a general.

"Good morning, Mr. Sherman," said Mr. Bunchley, drawing the door open smoothly with his left hand, his right hand held palm up and slightly out, in a single gesture that both presented Mr. Sherman to the world, and showed the world that

Mr. Sherman was a resident of this building, whose doorman would protect him, in case the world had any funny ideas.

"Good morning," said Mr. Sherman. Having expected the new doorman to know his name, Mr. Sherman stopped, realizing that he didn't know the doorman's. "You're new, aren't you?"

"Yes, sir."

"And your name is?"

"Darren Bunchley, sir."

"Thank you, Bunchley."

In the evening, when our fourth grader, Victoria Wurtz, came home from school, Mr. Bunchley moved briskly but evenly, his torso erect, his head still, from the center of the lobby to the door, reached his left arm across his chest, grasped the ornate handle and pushed, passed through the doorway with exactly four steps, pirouetting slowly one half turn as he did, and finished with his right foot at a forty-five degree angle from his left, which stood six inches from the now open door.

"Good evening, Miss Victoria."

"Good evening, Mr. Bunchley."

The above exchanges, occurring as they did on Mr. Bunchley's first day, make obvious the next must-have for any proper doorman, that is, a brilliant memory for names and faces. This is so essential when welcoming grandparents and grandchildren in ("You must be very proud, Mrs. Zeebruggen") and when escorting burglars out ("Nice try, wise guy").

It nearly goes without saying that a doorman must possess the skill, so mysterious to the out-of-towner, of being able to spot a taxicab four blocks away and by sheer willpower make it stop in front of his building and no other.

Mr. Bunchley never yelled (good heavens, no), never whistled (unthinkable), never ran into the street (out of the question). He merely lifted his index finger like so, not fully straight but with a conviction that always produced a taxicab in under twenty seconds.

"Here's one going downtown, Mr. Pearl."

"Thank you, Bunchley."

A doorman must be able to carry odd-shaped packages ("A striking piece, Mrs. Matisse") and willing to hold dogs on a leash when a resident has forgotten something in her apartment ("Sit, Winston").

Speaking of a doorman and his duties philosophically for a moment—or a doorwoman and her duties!—he or she must project a kind of authority, which, when summoned in full, will be the supreme authority in the building. After all, it is the doorman who is the first decider of who comes in and who goes out. He will always have the best interests of the building in mind, of course. Residents come and residents go, but the building remains. Where does this authority come from? Is it how his hat is tilted? Is it the circumference of his large overcoat when fully buttoned? Or is it the turn of his wrist when he holds aloft the large black umbrella over the open taxicab door in the rain? Perhaps all of these things. We, who live here, do not know. We only know whether our doorman has it or not.

Mr. Bunchley had it. We could all see that.

However, there was one essential duty, or we may say skill or gift, which every good doorman must have and which Mr. Bunchley lacked, and he knew it.

"What do you think the Yankees' chances are tonight, Bunchley?" said Mr. Sherman.

"Chances at what, sir?" said Mr. Bunchley.

"Mr. Bunchley, I just adore Mickey Mantle," said Miss Victoria.

"A classmate of yours?" said Mr. Bunchley.

"Do you think we should go with a right-hander or a left-hander against the Indians, Bunchley?" said the oldest resident.

"Surely both hands would be required," said Mr. Bunchley.

The oldest resident just grunted.

In other words, Mr. Bunchley could not talk baseball.

"Bunchley!" said the building manager. "See me in my office."

The building manager, putting down a sheaf of papers detailing the new city sidewalk cement-to-concrete ratio codes, looked sternly across his desk at Mr. Bunchley. He said, "Bunchley, have a seat."

Mr. Bunchley sat.

"You've been at 777 a month now."

"Yes, sir," said Mr. Bunchley.

"Your door opening is good."

"Thank you, sir."

"Your taxicab hailing is excellent."

"I do my best, sir."

"Package carrying, leash holding, name remembering, burglar ejecting—I have no complaints, couldn't be better."

"I'm glad, sir."

"You have a kind of presence, a certain something that we like."

"Thank you, sir."

"But there's one area where you're striking out," said the building manager, spreading his arms wide as if to a crowd. The building manager stood.

"Excuse me, sir?"

"Striking out! You know. Missing it. Not connecting." He walked around the desk and sat on the edge of it, facing Mr. Bunchley in his chair.

"How do you mean, sir?" said Mr. Bunchley.

"Baseball, Bunchley, baseball!" said the building manager. "Every doorman in every building on Garden Avenue can talk baseball for hours at a time to every resident, mail carrier, and cop on the beat. Except you."

"I'm sorry, sir."

"Bunchley, I'm going to give you two weeks to learn how to talk baseball. But if after two weeks you still can't talk baseball, it'll be three strikes and you're…"

"I'm what, sir?"

"OUT!" The building manager's thumb made that hooking motion over his shoulder that so many of us comprehend. Only Mr. Bunchley continued to be quite dumbfounded.

That weekend and all through the next week Mr. Bunchley read the sports section diligently, memorizing the box scores. He read baseball histories and biographies. He listened to sports radio over his early breakfast. And yet.

"Do you think Hector should pitch on only three nights of rest, Bunchley?" said Mr. Sherman, the following Monday.

"Three nights seems like an awfully long time to sleep between jobs," said Mr. Bunchley.

"I think they played Rockmorten too deep last night, Mr. Bunchley," said Miss Victoria.

"Were they fishing?" said Mr. Bunchley.

"I like to see a screwball, Bunchley," said the oldest resident.

"I like comedies, too, sir," said Mr. Bunchley.

The oldest resident just grunted.

For the remainder of that week Mr. Bunchley redoubled his efforts. He studied documentary films from the library. He watched highlight clips on various fan sites on the Internet. He traveled to Brooklyn to see the Cyclones play, buying their program, eating their hot dogs, and cheering with his neighbors in the bleachers whenever it seemed appropriate. But even so, he knew he couldn't manage it on his own account. Perhaps he couldn't quite see the point.

On Monday morning, the building manager said, "Bunchley, if you don't pull up your socks and keep your eye on the ball, come Friday—you'rrrrrrrrrrrrrrrrrrrrrrrrre OUT!"

All that day, Mr. Bunchley's door opening, taxicab hailing, package carrying, name remembering, and burglar ejecting were only competent, nothing special. They lacked vim. Mr. Bunchley's shoulders were down. His essential doormanishness was slowly seeping out at the back of his well-polished wingtips.

Mr. Bunchley sat moodily in the employee's break room in the basement. With his tea steeping in his own special cup, Mr. Bunchley pulled from inside his coat the twice-folded copy of *The Baseball Gazette*, smoothing it on the Formica tabletop. He paged through slowly, letting his eyes skip across the glossy spreads filled with analyses of seemingly limitless depth, with charts and statistics, with photographs. With a loud snort, which was about as close as Mr. Bunchley ever came to pronouncing an obscenity, he closed the magazine. He removed the tea bag from his cup. He let his eyes travel nostalgically around the room, from the teal-painted wall to the oversize calendar to the row of metal lockers. He stood, picked up *The Baseball Gazette*, and placed it neatly in the recycling box. Then, from his locker, he removed a small pamphlet entitled "Begonias: Is Their Time at Hand?" He returned with this publication to the table where he added a splash of milk and a dash of sugar to his tea.

At about the same time, on the nineteenth floor, Theo, one of our middle schoolers, pushed himself away from the essay he was writing concerning "What Would Jane Austen Choose as Her Favorite Social Media [sic] if She were a Teenager Today?" He stood and walked to the window to admire the six pots of carnations he was tending there. Turning away, he left his room, calling to his mother that he was going for a walk, that he needed to clear his head.

Returning to the building half an hour later, Theo found Mr. Bunchley on the curb looking precisely like a wilted begonia.

"What's the matter, Mr. Bunchley?" he said.

"This is my last week at 777," said Mr. Bunchley, kicking a gloomy pebble into the gutter.

"Really? How come?"

"I can't talk baseball."

"Neither can I," said Theo. As Theo pulled open the heavy door that Mr. Bunchley had neglected to hold open for him, he paused. He put a hand to his chin.

Mr. Bunchley, coming to himself, leaped to the door to hold it for Theo.

"Thank you, Mr. Bunchley. I think I know a way to cheer us both up. I'll be right back."

Theo returned carrying a tall, potted, red-and-white striped carnation.

"A Painted Lady!" said Mr. Bunchley. "Why, it's magnificent."

"I grew it from seed myself," said Theo.

"Let's put it here on the windowsill," said Mr. Bunchley.

For the first time that day Mr. Bunchley smiled. And so did Theo.

The next morning, when Theo came down to the lobby (the essay in his backpack), Mr. Bunchley had a surprise for him.

"A Laced Pink!" said Theo. "Let's put it next to the Painted Lady. Do you have more?"

"Oh, lots. I have my own little greenhouse."

And so it proved. The following day, Mr. Bunchley brought to the lobby a New Flame and a Phoenix, and Theo brought down a Duchess of Dorset and an Enchantress, and all were put on the windowsill.

The residents were enchanted.

"What a marvelous flower, Bunchley," said Mrs. MacDougal, stopping at the windowsill with her shopping.

"A Rob Roy," said Mr. Bunchley. "Drinks water like a fish and wants just a touch of bone meal."

"Magnificent, Bunchley," said Mr. Leonard. "What is it?"

"A Magnificent," said Mr. Bunchley. "Very hard to know where to find good seeds. But I know, I know."

"What's this then?" said the oldest resident.

"A Staffordshire Hero," said Mr. Bunchley. "One of Theo's. It's still early, I know, but it looks to me like Theo is going to have a very good season."

The oldest resident just grunted.

In the midst of all these new blooms, on Wednesday morning the building manager arrived and it was soon clear to Mr. Bunchley that his future hung in the balance. He stepped up to the building manager, knocked a little dust off his epaulets, placed his left hand into his right, and waited for whatever the building manager would throw at him.

"Bunchley, what's a foul ball?"

Mr. Bunchley answered, "An egg?"

"Strike one!"

On Thursday morning, the procedure was repeated.

"Bunchley, who's Babe Ruth?"

Mr. Bunchley answered, "Is this a trick question?"

"Strike two!"

On Friday morning, the building manager leaned back and fired from the bottom of his tonsils, "Bunchley, how many balls make a walk?"

Mr. Bunchley answered, "I'm sorry, sir, but you're speaking gibberish."

"Bunchley, you'rrrrrrrrrrrrrrrrrrrrrrre OUT!" And the building manager jerked his thumb over his shoulder.

You might think that Mr. Bunchley would have acted like a devastated man. That he might mope, or rattle all the little doors in the mail room, or even throw his braided cap into a potted palm. But no. On his last day on the job, Mr. Bunchley couldn't help feeling happy, simply because he was surrounded by the flowers he loved.

Mr. Bunchley smiled as he opened doors, hummed as he hailed taxicabs, and even made little pleasantries as he ejected burglars.

He was daydreaming happily about the new seed catalog that had arrived the day before when the elevator door opened and an old lady in a wheelchair rolled out creakily. It was Mrs. Rotterdam-Bottom, the owner of the building, who had not been seen in the lobby for thirty years.

"Who put all these flowers in my building?" demanded old Mrs. Rotterdam-Bottom.

"I did, ma'am," said Mr. Bunchley, "and Theo."

Old Mrs. Rotterdam-Bottom wheeled over to the windows to have a closer look.

"They're marvelous!" said old Mrs. Rotterdam-Bottom. "Why, I could smell the difference all the way up in my penthouse. Young man, what is your name?"

"Mr. Bunchley, ma'am."

"Mr. Bunchley, I'm giving you a raise."

"Thank you, ma'am. But I'm afraid you can't. You see, I've just been fired."

"Where's my building manager?" shouted old Mrs. Rotterdam-Bottom.

And so Mr. Bunchley was not fired after all. He opened doors, hailed taxicabs, carried packages, welcomed grandparents and grandchildren, and ejected burglars. And he never learned to talk baseball.

The residents got used to this.

One morning the next fall, Mr. Bunchley stayed in bed with a cold, but he sent along a new potful of carnations with Mr. Fouline, his temporary replacement.

When Theo saw these flowers in the lobby, he stopped to ask Mr. Fouline a question.

"Would you call those Purple Bizarres or Scarlet Flakes?"

Mr. Fouline said, "I wouldn't call them anything. I can't talk flowers."

Theo just grunted.

FRED AND THE PIGEONS

THEO WAS removing the few drooping petals from an otherwise glowing Noble Redeemer when from somewhere behind his left ear a voice boomed, "Ha!"

Theo began picking up the petals, which had scattered across the floor when he'd leaped two feet off the ground. He said, "Hi, Fred," and turned to see a smiling man standing patiently behind him.

Fred had lived at 777 Garden Avenue since, well, forever, as far as Theo was concerned—and as far as most of the other residents of the building were concerned, too. Looking at him, you might guess that he was thirty-five years old and had lived a very hard life or, alternatively, that he was sixty-five years old and had lived a very easy life. His skin was papery but his muscles were toned. His eyes were clear but had a faraway look. Certainly, he had great bunches of pencil-gray hair sprouting from the top of his head, the back of his neck, his ears, his chin, his nose, and above the top button of the plaid shirts he liked to wear. He peered at you through thick black-frame glasses. It was, however, definitely known that he had been in some kind of war; which war was not known. Whatever war it was, it was no doubt a loud one, as Fred began most conversations with a kind of verbal explosion. Usually it was his unmistakable "Ha!"—the hand grenade of his rhetorical arsenal.

"Ha!" said Fred again. "The gravity, Theo, the gravity! It's too strong today."

Together they walked to the front doors.

"I was wondering how the gravity was today," said Theo.

"Much, much too strong!"

Fred moved slowly through the door held open for him by Mr. Bunchley. Theo, following, smiled at the wink Mr. Bunchley gave him.

On the sidewalk, Fred stopped, tilted his head well back, and with his hands on his hips, breathed in deeply.

"That's better," he said. "The air's good today. Very good. Not too sweet and not too salty. Right amount of minerals too, and I put the AQI, that's the Air Quality Index, in case you're asking, at forty-two. But that could change. There's a lot of activity there, a lot of activity. We'll have to watch that. But it's the gravity that really needs attending to. First and foremost! We've got to bring it down. Are you coming with me on my rounds?"

"I can't today, Fred," said Theo. "I've promised Mr. Bunchley to help him with some replanting later on."

"Ho! Ho! Replanting! Digging! Moving! Moving plants! Displacing dirt! Digging dirt! Moving dirt! Moving dug dirt! Dirty dogs. Dirty hands! Hands across the sea! Ho! Ho!" Fred, continuing loudly in this way, turned and moved slowly down Garden Avenue. Theo watched him walk to the end of the block, where, stopping at the corner, he peered into the large trash can. Fred reached deep inside and pulled out a plastic container, which he opened and looked into carefully.

Theo waved, unseen, and then passed through the doors into the lobby.

Back at the corner, Fred examined the contents of the plastic container. By his estimate, it held three ounces of pasta salad, two ounces of garden salad, an ounce or so of salad dressing, and at least two ounces of a half-eaten hard roll—about half a pound of food. Removing just the hard roll, Fred closed the container and returned it to the trash. He placed the hard roll in a plastic painter's bucket, which was slung over his shoulder with a long leather strap.

"Onward!" said Fred.

It was Fred's habit, on three afternoons out of seven, to sample the city's trash cans, collecting from them bread, buns, pastries—anything made from grain. Up and down Garden Avenue he went, or Lexington, or even Park, starting from our building at Seventy-seventh Street, traveling as far uptown as Ninety-sixth, and as far down as Forty-second Street. Rain did not deter Fred. Nor did cold. On the normally hot days of summer Fred went shirtless. On the especially hot days Fred tied knots in the corners of his handkerchief, filled the resulting vessel with water from any ornamental fountain, and slapped it on his head.

Our city accepts most spectacles on its streets with equanimity, that is, without much comment. But Fred stood out.

Expensively dressed women turned their noses away from him as he passed. Children on scooters stopped briefly to watch him at his work and then rolled on. The doormen of the avenue, who knew Fred well, smirked or shouted a mocking "Hey, Fred. How's the gravity?"

On this particular day, a particularly hot one, Fred returned with only a half-full bucket of gatherings. Mr. Bunchley handed a glass of water to him.

"Thank you, Mr. Bunchley," said Fred.

"Hot day," said Mr. Bunchley.

"The gravity. The gravity," Fred said weakly. "I've got to lie down now, but then I'll deal with it first thing. Tell Theo that if he wants to come along and help, I'll be going out again after I've had my Postum at four."

"It is an outrage and a disgrace, and what's even worse," said Mrs. MacDougal, "I fear that it could be damaging to the value of our property here at 777."

Mrs. MacDougal stood at the building manager's desk. The building manager stared at the single large golden button on Mrs. MacDougal's blouse, which, like a UFO in a solar storm, heaved and bucked with every breath and every word that Mrs. MacDougal either drew in or spat out. He rubbed the top of his forehead with the first and second fingers of his right hand. With a sigh, he let his eyes travel up Mrs. MacDougal's blousy form in a determined attempt to meet her gaze. But this gaze was beamed not at the building manager but along Mrs. MacDougal's up-turned nose, into some vague middle distance.

She continued, "I know that Fred Adams has been a resident here for many years—"

"Since long before you arrived," said the building manager almost to himself.

"—nevertheless, this is no reason to allow him to tarnish the reputation of this building. We must put a stop to it."

"A stop to what, Mrs. MacDougal?"

"Why, don't be such an obtuse little man! You know that to which I refer. Fred's walking up and down Garden Avenue and all over our valuable neighborhood collecting food out of trash cans. Trash cans! Has the man no shame?" At this she snapped her head so forcefully in order to look hard at the building manager that the half-moon glasses she sometimes wore on a chain leapt off her nose and then swung helplessly, like a hanged man, on her chest.

"And he sometimes is to be seen in our very lobby without a shirt! Disgusting!"

"Look, Mrs. MacDougal, I don't like him any more than you do. He gives me a pain. Every time he opens his mouth I want to stick a sock in it. I got enough to worry about without him and his gravity. Sheesh! Have a seat, Mrs. MacD."

"I prefer to stand, thank you."

The building manager twisted a large fat finger back and forth in his ear.

"Listen. If I could get rid of him, I would. Like a shot. But he hasn't done anything wrong. Technically-like. He hasn't committed any crimes! If only he'd rob a store or something, then we'd have him!"

"He has already committed enough crimes against good taste to be convicted by any sane body of persons. He need commit nothing more. Can't you simply make it plain to him that this is not a proper residence for him?"

"What do you suggest?"

"Turn off his water or something."

"Oh, I couldn't do that." The building manager removed his finger from inside his ear and then scratched at the nape of his neck. "But maybe I could slow it down a little."

Mrs. MacDougal pulled her lips together like she was sucking a tiny straw, nodded, and left.

Theo and Fred quietly sipped their hot drinks and nibbled Fig Newtons.

"Ha!"

"Fred?"

"Theo!"

"Fred."

"The gravity's worse! I can feel it. It's getting me down. Don't you feel it?"

"Not really, Fred."

"I've got to get to work! Can't sit around all day. Where are my pants?"

"On the bed, Fred."

"On the bed, Fred! Standing on my head, instead! Ha! I stuck a spoon into Ted, he bled, saw red, I fled! Ha! Ha! Ha!" Fred hopped on one leg as he tried to insert the other into a terribly stained pair of khaki shorts.

"There, that's done it," he said, coming to rest.

He then moved toward the back corner of his room, shifting stacks of books and bric-a-brac as he went, bric-a-brac that seemed almost to lean in his direction, as if begging for attention.

"Not now," said Fred.

At the back, Fred lifted a three-string guitar from the lid of a barrel and then removed the lid. Taking a ladle from a nail on the wall, he dipped it into the barrel and pulled out a large dollop of brown lumpy pudding.

"The bread mash!" he said. Taking his bucket from another nail, he plopped in the mash. He added a couple more spoonfuls.

"Should be sufficient," he said.

Fred replaced the lid and guitar. Choosing a large spoon from a dusty metal bracket and slipping it into his breast pocket, he said, "Let's go."

"Off to feed the pigeons?" said Theo.

"More to the point, we're off to fix the gravity. Ha!"

On the sidewalk, the air had cooled somewhat.

Fred squinted up at the sky.

"It's just what I thought."

"What do you mean? I don't see anything. Nothing's happening."

"Precisely. Exactly. You have put your finger on it." Fred began to walk along the avenue. "Bingo. One hundred percent. You win a cigar."

"What?"

"Don't you see?"

"I don't see anything."

"Exactly."

"What?"

"What don't you see, exactly?" Fred had slung the bucket over his shoulder and was now tapping the spoon against it as they walked.

"What? Exactly. I exactly don't see."

"Must I spell it out for you? P-I-G-E-O-N-S. Pigeons. You don't see any pigeons. And I'll tell you why you don't see any pigeons. They're moping." Fred looked at Theo. "And that's what's causing the problems with the gravity. Ha!"

Up in apartment 15B, Mrs. MacDougal, wearing white cotton gloves, dusted her vases. Mrs. MacDougal's vases were her pride and joy, as they say, and occupied three long shelves stretching across her entire living-room wall. The vases of colored glass, some cut and faceted, others blown into swooping zoomorphic forms, stood near the windows where they could play with the sunlight—catching it, throwing it, absorbing it, fracturing it, in hushed, always changing ways. Farther from the windows stood the vases of ceramic, many frosted in glazes so delicate that Mrs. MacDougal rightly feared the gentlest sunlight might dim them or even crack them. The very farthest end of the shelves was reserved for the antique vases, some of them hundreds of years old, mostly Chinese.

Mrs. MacDougal replaced a flaring octagonal vase, in mustard yellow, of the art nouveau era, to its accustomed spot.

"There now," she said. "Isn't that better. All clean." She backed away from the wall of shelves, all the while gazing at her treasures. She leaned against the arm of her long sofa. Sighing, she said, "If anything happened to my babies, I think I'd just die!"

"You see, Theo, the force of gravity, as we feel it, is not a fixed thing. It's not a number that doesn't change. It changes plenty!" Fred removed his heavy glasses, coughed on them, wiped them on his filthy shorts, and then placed them back on his knobby nose. "Mostly it's in response to the particular distribution of mass on the earth's surface for any particular area that determines the gravity. Over the whole face of the globe on average gravity stays about even, sure. But at individual locales it varies enormously."

They crossed over to Lexington Avenue, Fred stirring the bread mash and occasionally waving the spoon to make a point.

"Here in New York City, we're particularly susceptible to variation because of all the buildings going up and coming down. Messing with the gravity!"

"Massing with the gravity, too," said Theo.

"Ha!"

"Making a mass."

"Ha! Ha! A big mass." Fred drew his eyebrows together. "But there is another force, a crucial force that is just powerful enough, fluid enough, and intelligent enough to counteract the fluctuations in local mass."

"Massive fluctuations?"

"Ha! And you know what it is?"

"What? What is it?"

"Pigeons."

"Wow. Pigeons?"

"Pigeons are what keep us steady. Pigeons are what keep these buildings from falling down all around us."

Fred let his spoon balance on the edge of the bucket and then teeter and fall into the bread mash.

"You might think that pigeons aren't massive enough to make much difference. Oh, but they are. Especially when they're in a flock and flying. Their combined mass is like a tiny hand on an enormous lever. By flying out and up over the city, and then wheeling and diving, a big flock can readjust any kinks in the gravity that some new skyscraper in midtown is causing. They're like gravity doctors constantly weaving the loose threads of gravity yarn back in place. Without them, anything could happen. Cyclones, tidal waves, even small earthquakes."

"I thought they were doctors, not weavers," said Theo.

"They're both."

"It's a mixed metaphor."

"Ha! Doesn't matter. The precise patterns they fly in are important though, of course." Fred smiled and looked far up, squinting into the sky over midtown. "But sometimes they mope."

"And that's where you come in?"

"And that's where *we* come in and here we are."

Over the last few blocks, Fred had led them to the right, to the west, coming to the bottom corner of Central Park where the Sherman Monument stood. Fred put his bucket down and pulled from the pocket of his shorts a small red rubber ball. He threw it up several feet into the air and caught it gently in his hand.

"Hmm, hmm, hmm," he said.

He threw it a little higher and caught it again. Then he held the ball at forehead height and dropped it. Theo ran to retrieve it from beneath the bushes where it careened.

As Theo crawled out, Fred said, "It's what I thought. The gravity's way off. Much too high. Let's get to work."

Fred put his thumb and forefinger in his mouth and let rip a mighty whistle blast that sent several families of tourists skittering away. Then he began hurling great spoonfuls of bread mash onto the tourist-free pavement. It took about three minutes, but only about three minutes, before the space around Fred and Theo, roughly the size of half a basketball court, was wall-to-wall pigeons: gray, blue-gray, bronze, black, white, piebald, big and little, but mostly big, pecking at the pavement, talking, shoving, laughing, and pecking at the pavement some more. Above, three times the number of pigeons that were on the ground flew in three enormous flocks, describing great arabesques in the air, banking, diving, settling in trees for a moment and then leaping up again, following their leaders—presumably ones with PhDs in gravity arts.

Fred and Theo sat on a bench and watched.

When the first flock of pigeons had dined to everyone's satisfaction, the second flock bellied up to the stones and Fred threw more of his delicious, one guessed, bread mash over their heads. And when the second flock finished and had wiped their mouths and excused themselves, the third and then the fourth flocks fell in and feasted. Throughout this feasting the cooing and scratching—small noises when coming from one pigeon—was a loud roar coming from the great mass.

Have you ever been in a school gymnasium that is also used as the cafeteria at lunchtime? The sound was a lot like that, only without the consonant sounds.

When the four flocks had all been fed, the pigeons left for a bit of after-dinner reflection. Some perambulated in twos and threes on the cobblestones. Most, however, sat quietly or fussed happily over their feathers in tree branches, on traffic-light stanchions, or, if they were really lucky, on the golden head of General Sherman on his golden horse.

"You see, Theo," said Fred, "they look happier already."

"How can you tell?"

"The eyes. It's in their eyes. It's not so much that they were hungry. It's more that they just wanted a little attention. They wanted to know we still cared."

The pigeons now became very quiet. The last murmuring cooer stopped murmuring. The strollers stopped strolling. A great stillness fell on that particular part of the city. When they themselves weren't making a racket, the pigeons' insulation, their feathers, worked like sound dampers, muffling much of the excess city noise.

Half of all the pigeons' eyes stared at Fred, half because each pigeon had turned his or her head, presenting a profile with a single golden, gray, blue, copper, or green eye fixed on the old man with the bucket.

Fred looked around once at the huge throng. Then, taking Theo's arm, he stood up, bringing Theo up with him.

Instantly, the pigeons rose up. The force of their wing beats buffeted the air and Theo's eardrums in a hundred thousand short shock waves. They flew up first slowly, then with more and more speed. How they didn't all tangle up with one another is a puzzle. The sound was like a helicopter, or a diesel locomotive—anything that concentrates a lot of power in a small place.

Maybe it was due to the noise, or to the way he stood up so quickly, but Theo was quite unsteady on his feet, feeling that either he or the pavement he was standing on was rocking.

The pigeons were flying in a huge cloud, the four flocks perfectly harmonizing in grand swoops and dives, towering climbs, and wide falling spirals.

Again, more than ever, Theo felt dizzy, the whole world around him was spinning and shifting. He clutched at Fred's arm.

"Don't worry," said Fred. "It's just the gravity readjusting. You feel it because we're standing right at the center of all the changes." He smiled at Theo, and then squinted back up at the sky and the pigeons.

After a minute and a half the great cloud of pigeons split into separate flocks, and then these dissolved into smaller flocklets, and doubles, and singles, and everyone traveled on to other parts of the city.

Fred sat back down lightly on the bench, stretching out his legs in front of him.

"Ah! That feels better," he said. "The gravity is right back down to normal. A healthy level."

Theo threw the red rubber ball hard onto the pavement, letting it bounce high into the hot evening air, and caught it.

Fred and Theo stepped into the September-cool of 777's lobby and stood a moment quite literally chilling.

"Look at you two!"

Mrs. MacDougal strode toward them from the direction of the building manager's office.

"This is disgraceful," she said. "You can't stand in the lobby like this, sweaty and malodorous and, ugh, you, Fred, without a shirt! It's unhygienical. It's in-aesthetical. It's anti-antiseptic. It's ... it's ... it's ... it's intolerable!"

The building manager now appeared at Mrs. MacDougal's side and spoke somewhat more quietly. "Fred, I would appreciate it if you did wear a shirt in the public areas of the building. It's common courtesy."

"Am I not wearing a shirt? Ha! I clean forgot. Ha! I'll put it right on."

Fred removed the bread-mash bucket from over his shoulder, placing it carefully on the polished floor. He pulled a crumpled plaid shirt from the pocket of his shorts, slipped it on, and began slowly buttoning it up.

"And what is in that bucket?" said Mrs. MacDougal. "I probably shouldn't ask."

"Pigeon mash. Well, bread mash, really. For the pigeons."

"Ugh!" Mrs. MacDougal staggered back. "For the pigeons!" Mrs. MacDougal stamped her foot. "That's enough! You are encouraging, aiding, abetting, condoning, and promoting the pigeon population. Vermin!" (It was unclear whether she meant the pigeons or Fred and Theo.) "The flying rats of this city. Fie! You should be poisoning the pigeons! You make me want to scream! It is people like you who give our great city its unfortunate reputation for filth!"

A gleam had come into Fred's eye, growing stronger as he buttoned each button, becoming a stabbing beam as he came to the last one.

"Don't you ever say anything about my pigeons. My pigeons! Besides Theo here, they're the best friends I've got!"

"I shouldn't wonder," said Mrs. MacDougal.

"The smallest, meekest, dumbest little pigeon sitting on the head of Christopher Columbus at Columbus Circle has more brains than you'll ever have!"

"There, there, Mr. Adams. Fighting in the lobby, I don't think so!" said the building manager. "Now that you got your shirt on, keep it on. And take your pigeon ma—whatever it is—upstairs to your room."

"Come on, Theo, let's go," said Fred.

"Mark my words, Fred Adams. I will have you removed from this building yet. I will consider it my duty to get you and your filth out of this building! It will be my duty!" shouted Mrs. MacDougal.

After Theo and Fred stepped inside the elevator, its doors closed softly but quickly, seemingly embarrassed at the scene in the lobby. As the elevator rose, Mrs. MacDougal's shouts grew fainter below them: "I'll get you yet! I'll get you yet!"

The years went by. The gravity went up and down but, thanks to Fred and the pigeons, the gravity never caused anyone any harm and did no damage.

One fall, a great hurricane threatened the city.

"What will happen to the pigeons?" said Theo, clutching his mug of Postum. "The paper says the winds will be over a hundred miles an hour."

"Oh, don't you worry about the pigeons," said Fred, with a chuckle. "They'll just see it as a healthy challenge. I won't be surprised if some of the younger lads don't spend the days surfing the front. Ha! Ha!"

Fred could see his joking wasn't making Theo feel less worried.

"Seriously, though, Theo. When it comes time for them to hunker down, they'll all find a sturdy perch and then once their feet are a-grippin' that perch, nothing can make them let go. Like steel! They'll be all right."

And the pigeons were all right. It took some parts of the city months to get over the storm, but the pigeons were up and about the day after the rain stopped. Fred was out on his rounds as soon as the mayor gave the all clear (actually a little before) to make sure everyone was looked after. Still, he really didn't need to. There was so much garbage—food to gobble—spilled onto the streets that the pigeons had a fine time.

Everyone survived in good balance.

Another worry loomed during Theo's last year at home. This time the storm didn't threaten the pigeons directly. It threatened Fred.

Mrs. MacDougal planned to introduce a new bylaw at the building's annual meeting which would require that each resident prove that he or she had a bank account with at least five thousand dollars in it.

"I can't raise that kind of money and she knows it!" said Fred. He and Theo sat dejectedly on a bench across from the statue of General Sherman.

Theo looked up at the statue and wondered if they could maybe scrape a little bit of the gold flake off, not so that anyone would notice but enough to put into a bank account for Fred.

"My pension is enough to keep me alive and pay my bills. But that's it. I don't have enough for a fancy bank account!"

For the first time he could recall, Theo thought his friend Fred looked really rattled.

"If she gets this thing through, I'm finished. I'm done for."

On the night of the meeting about half of the residents of 777—just enough to pass a new bylaw—were in the lobby, standing, sitting, and leaning against the pillars.

Mrs. MacDougal spoke for fifteen minutes. She spoke gracefully, calmly, and with such a reasonable air that she made it clear that anyone who opposed the new bylaw must be mentally unstable, bad, or, at best, some kind of criminal. Many residents were nodding at her and one another as she spoke. It was important for the health of the building. Sure. It was common sense. It was the right thing to do.

Fred stood next to the door to the stairs, looking small and frightened. For once, he had nothing to say. You could see the fighting sparkle drain out of his eyes. And as it did, Theo could see the fire in Mrs. MacDougal's eyes grow brighter and brighter.

When at last Mrs. MacDougal sat down in one of the leather lobby chairs, the building manager stepped in front. "Are there any other comments?" he said. You could tell that he felt sure that no one would dare speak against the proposal.

He looked a little less pleased, a little annoyed, when Theo pushed through the crowd to the front and stood next to him.

"I'd like to say something," said Theo.

"Go ahead, Theo," said the building manager. "I'm sure we'd all like hear what you have to say." He smirked.

Theo coughed into his fist.

He said, "It seems to me that this rule is just a bully rule. It's a rule to bully out all the poor people. And all the small people. I don't have five thousand dollars in a bank account. I still live with my parents. Some kids do have that kind of money. But I don't. Does this mean that I'm going to have to leave?"

"Oh, no, kid. Of course not," said the building manager. "This isn't meant to get you out. It's meant to get out the people we don't like!"

"Oh ho!" said Theo. "You admit it! This isn't about being reasonable. This isn't about doing the right thing for the building. This is about getting the people out that you don't like! You're the building manager. Not the building dictator!"

There was a lot of back and forth after that. The building manager turned bright red. Mrs. MacDougal slapped the arm of the leather chair quite a lot. And over the hubbub, Theo's voice rang out, "You don't even know what you're playing with. If you get rid of Fred, the whole building could be in danger. If the gravity isn't taken care of, who knows what could fall down?"

In the end, the new bylaw failed to pass by two votes.

The gravity was safe for the moment.

Theo continued to go on Fred's rounds whenever he was home from college. By the time Theo was a senior, he couldn't help notice that Fred was slowing down just a bit. That "Ha!" of Fred's that used to shake the ferns in the lobby now sounded more like "Heh" and it barely made an African violet tremble. Theo hardly ever jumped in surprise anymore.

At the end of his college days, Theo went off to do graduate work in New England. He had an awful lot of reading to do there, so he almost didn't have time to think about how Fred, the pigeons, and the gravity in New York were all doing.

Then one cold fall day Theo got a letter from Mr. Bunchley. This is what it said.

Dear Theo,

I'm so sorry to tell you that Fred Adams has left the building. I mean, he's moved on. I mean, Fred is dead! Sorry. I mean, he's gone to another world, maybe to a doorman building in the sky. Some of us will miss him, and I know you are one.

The funeral was last Saturday.

Always holding the door open for you,

Darren Bunchley

Included with this letter was the obituary that had appeared in The New York Times. In it was the answer to our question about whether Fred was a young man who had led a hard life or an old man who had led an easy life.

However, first, you need to hear a few words about how Fred died.

When Fred left this earth for that place where no gravity reaches, possibly carried there by the pigeons he loved, he went quietly and alone. Mr. Bunchley had noticed something wrong when for an entire day the calm of the lobby had not been broken by a single soft "Heh," however, he hadn't worried much about it. When two days passed, he did worry, and then in the evening of the third day, Mr. Bunchley, along with our superintendent, Oskar, knocked on Fred's door. And when there was no answer, Oskar let them in with Fred's extra key.

Theo looked at the picture of Fred in The New York Times. There he was, standing on the top step of a rolling ladder, about to climb into the cockpit of a Lockheed Martin X-35, the experimental supersonic jet. He looked young, handsome, proud. His eyes sparkled and his clean-shaven chin was square and daring. Theo quickly scanned the article. The air force was conducting tests on the change of the force of gravity over various altitudes and latitudes of the earth. Fred was their most fearless pilot, taking the tests higher and farther than ever before until his last mission, when the tail of his aircraft had exploded, hurling bits of plane in every direction. Fred had apparently blacked out for several seconds but not before he had initiated the escape protocols. His parachute had landed him on the northern slopes of Greenland. He fought the elements for a week before he stumbled into an Inuit village, where the local medical people had brought him back to health.

When he at last returned to his flight base in the Upper Peninsula of Michigan, his fellow pilots didn't know him. He had aged fifty years in a month.

Fred Adams had retired from the air force on a hero's pension and lived the rest of his life quietly and unrecognized at 777 Garden Avenue on the Upper East Side of Manhattan.

Theo put the paper down. He placed his chin in his left

hand and looked out the window to the clouds where he thought Fred's spirit might have gone. He wondered about Fred and what effect his death would have at home.

If Theo had seen the paper again three days later this last question about Fred might have been answered by two small items in the Metropolitan Section. In the first, an apparently unexplained mass bird event occurred over the course of a week on the Upper East Side. Residents expressed annoyance and consternation at the huge concentration of pigeons that seemed to have descended on the city, particularly on the benches, lampposts, marquees, ledges, and rooftops surrounding Seventy-seventh Street and Garden Avenue.

"The cooing was driving us nuts. I mean, we're used to pigeons, but this was like nothing I ever heard," the building manager at 777 Garden Avenue is quoted as saying.

Then after a week of cooing, squatting, and milling about, the pigeons left as mysteriously as they arrived, taking flight in a gargantuan gray mass, circling twice and vanishing.

"It was eerie," said Mr. Bunchley, 777 Garden Avenue's doorman.

According to Eugene Pinion, an ornithologist with the Parks Department, scientists are baffled. "Maybe it has something to do with the stars," he said.

The second item was very brief.

A tremor, a small earthquake, not unheard of in New York, occurred Tuesday afternoon, centered on the Upper East Side of Manhattan. Some minor damage was reported.

No, Mrs. MacDougal never got him.

Quite the contrary.

At seventeen minutes after two in the afternoon on Tuesday, the day of that small earthquake, Mrs. MacDougal stood with her back against the arm of her living-room sofa, and watched as, singly or in pairs, or threesomes, every one of her vases tottered, tilted, and then fell to the floor, smashing into perhaps millions of pieces. Hundreds of thousands, anyway, without a doubt.

The Opera Singer Inspection

As EVERYONE who lives in New York City knows, each building must have at least one working opera singer. Each residential building, at any rate. It's a fact—part of the fabric of the city.

New Yorkers like to come home in the evenings, spring through fall, suffering perhaps from the troubled thoughts of the day, to have these troubled thoughts dispelled by cerulean melodies floating down upon them, like heavenly soot. Maybe it is an aria from *La clemenza di Tito* by Mozart, or maybe it is one of the parts of the chorus of *Otello* by Verdi, or maybe it is merely the singing of scales and arpeggios. But these melodies, even when they occupy only half of half of an ear, have become essential to the New Yorker's life. And this is true even if we hate opera, and some of us do. Still, we need opera singers. Few of us know precisely from which apartment the notes waft down. But we know and count upon the fact that there will be notes wafting down from one little apartment in every corner of the city.

It is now law, codified sometime during the 1930s under

Mayor La Guardia. The city ordinance was passed nearly unanimously—there was a small but tenacious anti-opera block, polka players and libertarians, mostly. Whether the opera singer is a soprano, alto, tenor, baritone, or bass, whether lyric, dramatic, heroic, or a member of the chorus, is, of course, left to the discretion of each building's board of directors.

This legislation, having been written so long ago, is now simply an accepted and expected part of everyday life. Every building must have an opera singer. We're speaking of buildings with five stories or more, or buildings with twenty or more units. Every New Yorker knows this.

But perhaps you live out of town and don't know this. Now you know.

However, what even many New Yorkers don't know is that these opera singers, from time to time, must be inspected.

This second law came about as the result of a famous tragedy that occurred in the 1960s.

An elderly gentleman, a banker named Brown, was returning to his home on the Upper West Side, lost in thoughts of the ratio of dollars to rubles in the wool industry, when he was struck by a falling high E. It came not from his own building's opera singer but from the opera singer next door, who was making such a hash of the Queen of the Night's aria from The Magic Flute, that when she came to the high E, it fell and struck Mr. Brown so hard in between the ears that it caused a massive brain hemorrhage and he died.

A tragedy all around. The opera singer felt terrible. She admitted later, when questioned by the police sergeant, that she was not in good form that day, that she had been out of practice.

Naturally, the incident was taken up by the city council, and the result of their many-weeks-long investigation was the drafting and pushing through of what has come to be known as Local Law 27, more commonly known as the Opera Singer Inspection.

We at 777 have had our opera singer now for many years. Unfortunately, they don't last forever, but ours has been going strong and shows no need for replacement. Still, when every five years the inspection rolls around we all get a little nervous. The costs of repairing or replacing an opera singer can be enormous and can lead to complicated financial obligations for the building. Something best avoided if possible.

Miss Myrna Murray-Burdett is our opera singer. She is a lyric soprano. Of course, we like to think that the best buildings have sopranos. Nothing wrong with a fine tenor, but a soprano gives the building just a little more polish. (The snobs at 740 Garden Avenue insist that the soprano must be a coloratura—the snobs!) Myrna is known for her wonderful Micaela, which brought such praise to her from all the people in Chattanooga who heard her in the role there. We've never had any trouble with her. Day in, day out, year in, year out, she runs her scales and arpeggios, and when her accompanist, Timothy Noon, sits down with her for selections from Der Freischütz or The Barber of Seville or La Traviata, we all breathe easier: The building has its opera singer.

That is, we have never had any trouble with our opera singer until last Sunday evening, exactly one week and a day before the Opera Singer Inspector was due to arrive.

Miss Myrna Murray-Burdett came in that evening on the arm of, well, actually, he was on her arm—she's a big woman —let's say she came into the lobby in the company of a new admirer. Naturally, she was aglow, beaming, effervescent to the point of bubbling over.

Miss Murray-Burdett said to Mr. Bunchley, "Bunchley, I'd like you to meet Mr. Caswell Grape."

"How do you do?" said Mr. Bunchley.

"I'm the biggest fan of Miss M.-B. She rocks my world!" said Mr. Grape.

"Oh, Cas!" said Miss M.-B. "You sound like a teenager!"

"I *feel* like a teenager. Have another mint?" Caswell, with a rakish smile on his face, pulled out from a brown paper bag a long, aqua-green box, which he held open toward Miss M.-B.

"Oh, Caswell, you *do* know the way to my heart," said Miss M.-B. and she took the mint, opening the wrapper with an easy twist and placing it delicately on the tip of her tongue, which then retreated instantly into her mouth like a shy chipmunk to its underground den.

"Mmm, hm, hm, hm, hee, hee, hee," she said, and they giggled, and nearly skipped over to the elevators.

After the elevator doors had closed, Mr. Bunchley said to the building manager, who was just crossing the lobby from his office with a clipboard under his arm, "They certainly seem in love."

"I don't care if they're in love, just friends, or hate each other with a passion, so long as she passes the Opera Singer Inspection, which happens one week from tomorrow." The building manager strode purposely from the lobby.

On Monday, Miss Myrna Murray-Burdett woke up with just the merest, teensiest bit of a something in the back of her throat, like one fly on a vast windshield, hardly worth mentioning, really.

"It's nothing," she said to herself.

That evening the fly felt more like a beetle. She gargled with salt water, took a hot shower, and went to bed.

Tuesday morning, Miss M.-B.'s throat definitely felt wrong. Still, she decided it was nothing to be worried about, and that she would simply blast it, whatever it was, out of her insides with some full-throated vocalizing. She sang loud—she might prefer that we said, *forte*—during her voice lesson. She sang louder—*piu forte*—in her afternoon rehearsal. And she sang her loudest—*forte fortissimo*—in the practice studio she sometimes used off Eighth Avenue, just before drinks with Caswell. By evening her throat felt awful.

"It's nothing serious, my love, is it?" said Caswell, holding her warm left hand in both of his. "Have a mint?"

Out came Miss M.-B.'s tongue and in went the mint. Then she gargled and went to bed.

By Wednesday the beetle had become a frog. Thursday it was a bullfrog, Friday morning it was a gigantic, prehistoric bullfrog, and by Saturday night, Miss M.-B.'s beautiful soprano voice sounded like some kind of ancient lawn mower biting a stump.

Earlier on that Saturday afternoon, the building manager had been pacing back and forth in the lobby.

"Bunchley," he said, "have you seen Miss Murray-Burdett today?"

"I have not seen Miss M.-B. in two days, sir."

"Two days! I hope to God she's just resting up." The building manager put his hand to his brow and began rubbing it strongly. "But you've heard her, right? Scales and stuff?"

"I have not heard her, sir. Would you like me to knock on her door and inquire as to how her vocal cords are doing?"

"Of course not, Bunchley!" The building manager began twirling the hair behind his ear. "Opera singers are temperamental! One false move, one moment where you show just a little less than total confidence in any opera singer, *especially sopranos*, and their insides go *kerflooey!* and they won't work properly for weeks. They're like boilers that way."

The building manager stopped twirling his hair and returned to pacing.

On Sunday morning, Miss M.-B. sat in her bed, opening and shutting her mouth like a goldfish of less than average intelligence, afraid to make any sound at all for fear of the horror that might come out.

There was a sharp tap at the door. Caswell opened it and the building manager strode in looking anxiously around. "Well, Miss Murray-Burdett, how are you today? I see you are still in bed, no doubt resting up for tomorrow's inspection. Good. Good. Glad to see it. Glad to see you are treating to-morrow's inspection with the proper seriousness it demands. Not that there is anything for you to worry about. Of course not. Just like always, you'll sail right through. Right through!"

The building manager put his hands together the way peo-ple do when they pray, he probably didn't even know he was doing this, and smiled at Miss M.-B. He waited for her to say something. He waggled his eyebrows at her and smiled some more.

Miss M.-B., however, said nothing. She just rolled the edge of her comforter back and forth between her fingers and opened her eyes wide at the building manager. She still said nothing, but inside she wondered what she would do if she lost her position as the building's opera singer. She couldn't think what she would do—it was unthinkable.

"Saving your voice for tomorrow, eh?" said the building manager. "Good. Good! I'll just be going then."

At last, Miss Myrna reached out her hand as the building manager was turning away, and held him by the arm.

When he turned to look at her, she said, that is, she mouthed, "I can't sing."

"You what?" said the building manager.

"I can't sing," she mouthed again. "I've lost my voice."

"You've lost your voice!" shouted the building manager.

Miss M.-B. clapped her hands to her ears and nodded fre-netically, wrinkling her forehead in shame and anger.

The building manager shook his hands at the ceiling and

shouted again, "She's lost her voice! And tomorrow is the Opera Singer Inspection!" (From a dramatic standpoint, the building manager might have made an excellent Verdi tenor.)

After this, there was a heavy silence, which was finally broken by Caswell, who said to no one in particular, "Mint?"

The rest of that Sunday passed in a storm of phone calls and house calls and calls to all of the musical gods in heaven. The building manager called Miss Murray-Burdett's doctor, the house doctor, and his own doctor. Each one had a different opinion. Next he called her voice coach, her life coach, and his son's Little League baseball coach. No help there, either.

"Time," wailed the building manager, "we don't have time!"

By nightfall, everyone was exhausted, at wit's end, and still there was no working soprano in the building.

It was a haggard building manager who accepted the chipper "Good morning!" from Mrs. MacDougal as she stepped out of the elevator.

"What's good about it?" he croaked.

Mrs. MacDougal was looking happy and healthy, just having returned from a week at her summer house in East Hampton, at the far eastern end of Long Island.

"Your trouble is you work too much. You need to spend a little time at the beach," said Mrs. MacDougal.

"No, my trouble is I got an opera singer what's got no voice, and an Opera Singer Inspector due to show up here sometime between one and five o'clock this afternoon. You know how these city inspectors don't give no exact time for showing up. Between one and five. Probably be here about seven."

"What is that you say? We have an opera singer with no

voice? What is the matter with Miss Murray-Burdett? She has never given us any trouble before."

"She ain't got no voice, and there's nothing doing about it." (The Brooklyn boy in our building manager always seems to emerge in times of stress.) "I had fifty guys in here yesterday looking at her from uptown to downtown, from indoors to the sidewalk, and they couldn't find nothing."

"Oh for heaven's sake," said Mrs. MacDougal, waving her hands next to her ears as if shooing flies. "I'm away from here for one little week and the place falls to pieces. Take me to her."

Caswell Grape opened the door hesitantly to Mrs. MacDougal's three forceful knocks.

"Don't you never go home?" said the building manager to Caswell as he pushed past him into the room.

Mrs. MacDougal surveyed the scene of Miss M.-B.'s studio apartment. Miss M.-B.'s several dressing gowns lay crumpled over the backs of her two chairs. Magazines, dog-eared and worn, were spread over most horizontal surfaces and these were covered by empty or nearly empty take-out food containers. And everywhere Mrs. MacDougal looked were the aqua-green boxes, now empty, of chocolate mints, like the dotted line on a treasure map, showing what had been the unswerving route Caswell had taken to Miss Murray-Burdett's heart.

Mrs. MacDougal moved her eyes, her head and body following slowly around, and when she completed the circle she folded her arms, glowered at poor Miss M.-B., and began tapping her foot.

"What have you got to say for yourself?" said Mrs. MacDougal sharply.

Miss M.-B. opened and closed her shapely mouth hopelessly. It was really pathetic to see it.

Mrs. MacDougal lifted an empty mints box and examined it, held at arm's length from her.

Miss M.-B. kept opening and closing her mouth.

Mrs. MacDougal placed the mints package down again, gently, smiled first at Miss M.-B., then at Caswell, and finally at the building manager.

At last, she turned to Caswell, who sat on the very edge of Miss M.-B.'s bed by her feet.

"And you are?" said Mrs. MacDougal to him. "No, let me guess." She smiled. "You are Miss Murray-Burdett's biggest fan."

Caswell nodded nervously.

"Her new admirer?" Mrs. MacDougal winked broadly. "You would do anything for Miss Murray-Burdett." The nodding was now constant. "Anything at all, to win her for yourself. And what better way to win her than to bring her something sweet? Mints, for instance?"

Caswell looked like a bobblehead doll on the dash of a car racing down a gravel road in Georgia.

A thick silence fell on the room, like a too-long breath between song phrases.

Then Mrs. MacDougal thundered, "Has no one ever heard of acid reflux around here?" She went on. "You've been poisoning our opera singer! Where did you meet this guy?" She wheeled on Miss Murray-Burdett, who merely looked large-eyed and miserable.

"Is he working for the building management at 740 or something?" She whipped back upon Caswell. "Are you?"

"No, no, no, no," said Caswell, now only shaking his head.

"Okay, listen up, lover boy. We've got approximately five hours to fix this. Here's what I want from you. Firstly, one gallon of whole milk. Secondly, two loaves of white bread. And thirdly, a bottle of Tums. Make it the opera-size. You can even make it the Wagnerian opera-size. Now, be back here with everything in twenty minutes or never show your face again!"

Mrs. MacDougal turned to Miss M.-B. as Caswell Grape scurried out the door.

"Have you got a toaster?"

Behind the closed door of Miss Murray-Burdett's apartment there was a lot of tearful murmuring until Mrs. MacDougal's voice was heard clearly and commandingly. "Shut it!" she said. "Save it for later."

The rest of the morning, for those closely involved, had all the tension of a hospital waiting room on the occasion of a first baby.

The building manager returned to pacing in the lobby, now with added vigor. Caswell, having procured the required items, hovered in the hall outside of Miss M.-B.'s door.

At ten o'clock, the door was wrenched open and Mrs. Mac-Dougal held out a crumpled burgundy evening dress along with a pair of black pumps.

"Get the dress cleaned, the shoes polished, and have it for us by noon."

As Caswell walked up the hall with the clean dress and shined shoes his heart did a double bump. In the quiet of the empty hallway he, her biggest and most remorseful fan, definitely could hear the stirrings of the true voice of Miss Murray-Burdett. That hideous frog was changing into the gorgeous princess it should be.

At one twenty-five, Mr. Bunchley walked through the front door to the lobby, announcing that the Opera Singer Inspector was a block away.

The office manager said a brief prayer and stepped out onto the sidewalk to meet him.

And just as the Opera Singer Inspector, a Mr. Celimontana originally from Milan, reached the door, the lilting passage from Bizet's *The Pearl Fishers*, act II, scene ii, floated down from somewhere above, not like celestial soot this time but like miraculous flakes of heavy summer snow.

Mr. Celimontana raised his fingers and thumb to his mouth and kissed them, and when he did his fingers sprang open as his hand fell away, like a blooming flower.

"*Brava*," he said, "*brava*." He smiled and nodded at the building manager, and added, "*Va bene*." (All is well.)

THE FORGOTTEN ROOM

THE BUILDING we live in, 777 Garden Avenue, was built in the second decade of the twentieth century, which makes it, as we are now in the twenty-first century, nearly a hundred. The building's centennial is coming up, and what a party we'll have.

Garden Avenue itself is approximately twice as old, having been laid out in the grand street plan of 1811. Like Manhattan Avenue of the West Side, which runs only from 100th Street to 125th Street, Garden Avenue is one of the short avenues, starting at Seventy-second and also ending at 125th, tucked in between Lexington Avenue and Third Avenue. And just like Manhattan Avenue, even many lifelong New Yorkers have never heard of it, exclaiming in surprise when they first, sometimes literally, stumble upon it.

However, some New York wags have scoffed at the avenue over the years, calling it Wannabe Park Avenue, or Poor Man's Park, or Park Avenue Lite. "What's next?" they say. "Backyard Avenue? Croquet Lawn Boulevard? Rolled Sod Drive?"

There may be some truth in this, but for those New Yorkers who live there (and have a little sense of humor) the avenue offers them a wonderful mix of the high and the low, the rare and the common, salmon tartare and a bagel with a schmear.

Number 777 was constructed at a time when large apartment buildings were taking over the avenues from downtown going up, knocking down and replacing the large family mansions, which were themselves at that time only about thirty years old. Still, times were changing in the city, many people were moving in, and the families in these mansions were selling their homes and either moving out or moving into the new buildings, sometimes into the very buildings standing on the bones of their old houses.

Naturally, this was a great time to be an architect. The architects of 777 were two gentlemen, Solomon Archer and Nathaniel Stone, of the firm Archer, Archer, Stone and Green. While Mr. Archer made sure the buildings were solid and unlikely to fall over, Mr. Stone saw to it that they looked good. Mr. Stone was a bit of a romantic, constantly falling in love with building styles of the past from all of history and from all over the world. Sometimes his designs looked like Aztec pyramids. Sometimes they looked like Egyptian palaces. And sometimes they looked like the tops of Gothic cathedrals. Mr. Stone had traveled a great deal as a young man—he grew up in Iowa—and always had a pencil and a book to draw in. The world became his department store. Having become a successful architect in New York, and traveling again, he might say, "I'll have that tower"—pointing to the top of an Italian palazzo—"on my building at Eighty-sixth and Lex." Or, "That Gothic entrance is just what I want for my apartments at

Broadway and 103rd." And he would busily draw everything in his sketchbook.

It then became Mr. Archer's somewhat tedious task to make it all fit.

Number 777 Garden Avenue is perhaps the grandest building Archer and Stone ever built together. At street level it rises right up out of the ground, sheer, with no hemming or hawing. There is no moat, or hedge, or black fence holding you away from the smooth pink granite walls that form the first two floors. There are no steps up into the lobby, nor is there a carriage turnaround. Mr. Stone may have been a romantic, but he knew that carriages were on their way out. One minute you stroll on the sidewalk, and the next minute you are through the doors and into the magnificent lobby.

Stylistically, you would have to call the whole thing neo-proto-Aztec-Egyptian-Gothic.

Mr. Stone really let himself go. Zigzaggy, smooth stone surrounds the exterior doors. Swoopy Egyptian columns with terra-cotta plumes hold up the lobby ceiling. And in the oddest places both inside and out, you'll come upon something vaguely Viking—maybe runes woven into the balustrade here, a dragon-headed downspout there.

The building goes up cleanly and evenly enough for twelve floors, as mentioned, but then breaks into all manner of ziggurat shapes—ziggurats are ancient zigzaggy pyramids—ending in a soaring tower that conceals the water tank. The odd setbacks created by the zigzagging shape allow for many strangely configured terraces on the top nine floors. In the courtyard, on the back side of the building, two three-story chimneys stand next to the central tower connected by flying arches, like a piece of a grand Roman aqueduct, just to mix things up even more.

Do you know your Norse sagas?

The top nine floors of 777 Garden Avenue are Nathaniel Stone's vivid imagining of what Valhalla, the palace of the dead Viking warriors, should look like.

Maybe you picture it differently.

Inside, Mr. Stone let his imagination run pretty freely, as well. While you aren't likely to be suddenly face-to-face with a grinning Viking-ship dragon head, like you might be on the outside, the layout of each floor is still kind of reptilian, if you can think of long, twisting hallways and weirdly shaped rooms in that way. Most of the floors two through twelve (there are no apartments on the ground floor) are divided into five, six, or seven apartments. Then floors fourteen through seventeen (there is no thirteen) into two, three, or four apartments, floors eighteen and nineteen have one apartment each, and the very top two floors, twenty and twenty-one, are combined into one duplex apartment. This is now the apartment of old Mrs. Rotterdam-Bottom, who owns the building—she is the granddaughter of Mr. Theophilus Rotterdam, who hired Mr. Archer and Mr. Stone in the first place.

Apartments were large and many-roomed when the building was new. Most families then still had people to help them, like a maid or a cook, and these helpers often had their own rooms in the apartment. Dumbwaiters, a small kind of hand-operated elevator, brought food and dishes from one floor to the next and laundry up from the basement. Apartments didn't have dishwashers, microwaves, or flat-screen TVs. Instead, they had maid's rooms, pantries, and nooks and crannies.

It was a comfortable, roomy life in the city at 777 Garden Avenue one hundred years ago.

In one of the grand, full-floor apartments, on the nineteenth floor to be exact, lived old Mr. Waterby, who had been there since the building's doors were first opened. In fact, his former mansion was the one that was knocked down to build 777 in the first place. He didn't much miss his old house. No, he preferred his airy apartment, the wonderful views down the avenues, the simpler living, no more fussing with the roof, and so on. He doted on his apartment. It had nineteen rooms: four bedrooms, a dining room, a living room, a library, maid's and cook's rooms, a front hall, a back hall, and so on. But Mr. Waterby's favorite room was at the back of the apartment, behind the elevator and stairs that run up through the center of the building. The music room. You entered the room by one of two doors, one north, one south, facing each other, which gave the room a certain formality. It was small, sun-filled. Then turning to the center of the room, where the piano stood, you faced west and the French doors that opened onto a narrow terrace, just big enough to hold the small audiences that attended the impromptu concerts Mrs. Waterby gave, seated at the piano with the French doors open.

The room itself seemed happy at this time—kind of glowing. But perhaps that was just a trick the light played, the light that came first from the setting sun and then from the shaded lamps, turned on one by one as the glow in the west faded.

Afterward, guests often said "The evening was magical!" and it did seem that way as the musical notes of Mrs. Waterby's gentle playing mingled with the distant sounds of the street below, while the thousands of lights in myriad tints came on beneath them. Somehow, perhaps because the maroon-and-blue sky was large, and the horizon was visible as a line of inky purple, it was said that the evening felt like being on a ship at high sea.

The room *was* magical.

Then, one fall, Mrs. Waterby died.

Mr. Waterby, while not a man to give in to despair, never having been described as dreamy—"I am not a sentimentalist," he would often say—nevertheless locked first the French doors to the terrace and then the two doors leading to the rest of the apartment, one north and one south, and never opened them again.

Years passed. Then a second misfortune befell Mr. Waterby, though not as great a misfortune as the first; the stock market crash of 1929.

He was not ruined, financially, but he was no longer quite so wealthy. Thus, in order to save a little money, and with Mr. Rotterdam's permission, he determined to split the apartment in half, then live in the north half and rent out the south.

Toward that end Mr. Waterby hired Solomon Archer's son, Benjamin, to draw up the plans and get the thing done. He, Mr. Waterby, would in the meantime spend the summer in his house on Fire Island.

Now it happened that Benjamin's parents had often been present at the music evenings at the Waterby home and Mrs. Archer always described them to Benjamin in detail and with rapturous admiration. Mr. Waterby's instructions were to split up the apartment evenly and to leave the existing rooms intact. Now, it is difficult to divide nineteen in half and come up with a whole number, which you know if you've tried it, so Benjamin Archer faced a dilemma.

"Well, it's obvious, isn't it," thought the young architect, "the nineteenth room, the music room, must go with Mr. Waterby in the north apartment." And so he drew up the plans accordingly.

However, Mr. Waterby, with his bags packed for Fire Island and waiting in the hall, gave his parting instructions to Frank Sebastiano, the building contractor.

"Put the music room with the other apartment. I'd rather not have it a part of mine. It reminds me too much of my dear wife," he said.

As the elevator doors closed, Mr. Waterby heard Mr. Sebastiano's chalky voice saying, "Yo—new plans. Close up the wall on the north side of that music room there. Mr. W. don't want it no more."

A month later, with the work progressing smoothly, Frank Sebastiano decided he could give himself a couple of days off for fishing from his boat in New Jersey. He called his buddy Joe and asked him to take over supervising the job. So the next morning, Joe arrived and was soon scratching his head over the plans. The work was nearly done, he could see that. He scratched his head again. The plans clearly indicated that the south door of the music room should be walled up, and it still stood open. Thinking that Frank had just not gotten around to doing it, he ordered the men to wall up the south door of the music room. The workmen, who were all Polish immigrants and didn't like arguing with the boss, especially not in their broken English, and who didn't mind so much one way or the other, with several shrugs walled up the south door as well, being careful not to wall up themselves or any tools inside. It is ironic or something that they were closing up a room that had once been filled with Polish music—Frédéric Chopin, the great Polish composer, was one of Mrs. Waterby's favorites.

And so both the north door and the south door of the music room were walled up.

Mr. Waterby returned at the end of the summer and happily paid Mr. Sebastiano's bill, having first checked that everything was to his liking, which it was. And a month later, a young family moved into the south-facing apartment and happily paid their first month's rent after having checked that everything was to their liking, which it was.

And that was that. The little room, the music room, was sealed. For some years, residents of 777 Garden Avenue remembered the little music room, especially Mr. Waterby. But no one spoke about it.

And then the little room was forgotten.

Years went by. Years and years and years went by. And then decades. Outside the room, life went on. Inside the room, life had stopped.

Dust, sneaking in through the cracks around the French doors, slowly piled in the corners. Paint and plaster cracked and then finally fell, breaking into bits hitting the floor, adding to the dust. When a loose paving stone in the terrace just above wasn't repaired right away, water seeped in, loosening plaster in the ceiling, pooling on the floor, making the beautiful oak parquet warp and break.

Only the piano remained mostly intact. It was a noble Steinway and its heavily coated hardwood repelled the dust and water valiantly.

Bit by bit, the room, which had always been happy, even when Mrs. Waterby had played tearful songs, maybe especially then, was now morose, thinking only of itself and its decay, not even remembering the former days of music. The whole room was depressed and silent. The world no longer cared for it. It no longer cared for the world.

Then, after three-quarters of a century of solitude and depression, the forgotten room sent out an S.O.S.

A little crack formed in one of the panes of glass of the French door. It started in the lower-left corner and crept up to the upper-right. Every day, the crack rose about half an inch. After thirty days, the crack reached the top. The forgotten room was not done, however. The room waited now for the fall and winter storms to rattle the windows. In November a tremendous storm howled down the Hudson from the north, and its winds whipped and flogged the building from every direction until it knocked out half of the cracked windowpane, the glazing that had held it in place having long ago become brittle and mostly fallen out of its frame. The glittering shards of glass lay on the terrace, leaving a black hole in the window.

The S.O.S. was sent. The little music room shrank back into itself and waited and hoped.

Jeremy's New Year's Day party was in full swing when Theo arrived. High-school-aged students, some recognized and some unrecognized by Theo, sprawled, holding various drinks and cookies, throughout the apartment. When an hour later, the clinking and shouting and thumping of the party just got to be too much for him, Theo stepped onto the quiet and cold of the apartment's terrace high up on the twentieth floor. A couple of other guests stood about as well.

Theo saw Edward from his class and walked over and leaned on the terrace railing next to him.

"Yo, Theo," said Edward.

"Hi," said Theo.

They stared off over the city for a bit.

"This is so awesome up here," said Edward.

"Yup."

Theo leaned out over the railing and shivered.

"You know, my building should be right over there somewhere," Theo said, pointing. "Jeremy's building is on Lexington, mine is on Garden, one block closer to the East River. And we're on the same block." Theo looked across the jumbled courtyard, trying to recognize the buildings by their unfamiliar back sides. "There it is!"

"Where?"

"There. The tall zigzaggy yellowy one with the chimneys. See which one I mean?"

"Yeah, that one. The goofy-looking one."

"Yup, that's my building. I wonder if I can find my apartment. Let's see, we're on the downtown side on the nineteenth floor. One, two, three, four..."

"This is the twentieth floor. Just count one down."

"Oh, yeah. Okay, that must be it. It is! It is! There's my mom's little pine tree on the terrace and my old bike."

Behind them the bright whitish winter sun was slowly descending on the short day, and its low slanting light lit up 777 Garden Avenue the way a member of the chorus line is lit on a Broadway stage. Never did the building look so yellow, so sparkly.

Really, thought Theo, it looked too sparkly.

"Oh my gosh! There's broken glass all over Miss Stickleback's terrace, and look, one of the French doors is broken."

"I think I see it!" said Edward. "I think I don't care!"

"I do! It's weird that Miss Stickleback hasn't fixed the window. I hope she's all right. I'm going to go home. I'm tired of the party anyway. I want to see if she's all right. Say good-bye to Jeremy for me, will you?"

"Okeydoke," said Edward, giving Theo the thumbs-up, and then returning to staring out over the city.

Half an hour later, Theo rang the bell to Miss Stickleback's apartment. Miss Stickleback was the great-granddaughter of the sister of old Mrs. Waterby. When Mr. Waterby had grown too old to live alone, his wife's niece and her husband had moved in to help him, and when he died, they stayed on. That was Miss Stickleback's grandmother.

When Miss Stickleback opened the door—first having called out, "Who is it?" and having heard Theo's shouted, "It's

Theo!"—Theo said, "Hello, Miss Stickleback. I just wanted to say that I noticed one of the panes of your French door is broken and there's glass on your back terrace. Didn't you know?"

"No, no, I didn't know that," said Miss Stickleback. "Come in, Theo. Now, let's take a look at this. First of all, I didn't know I *had* a back terrace. Would you like a glass of milk or something? Tea?"

"A glass of milk would be great. I've just had a lot of chocolate, plus chocolate cookies at a friend's house. By the way, Happy New Year, Miss Stickleback."

"Thank you, Theo, and same to you. Here is your milk." By now they were both sitting at Miss Stickleback's small kitchen table. Miss Stickleback folded her hands in front of her and said, "Now what's all this about a back terrace?"

"Well, I was at this friend's party I was telling you about. He lives on Lexington, on the twentieth floor, straight over from us. And I was on his terrace, looking at our building. I counted the floors up, and then down, and I found our floor. And I was showing my friend Edward. And I said, 'Hey! There's a broken window on Miss Stickleback's back terrace!' Then I thought I'd come here and tell you."

"But as I just recently mentioned, I don't have a back terrace."

"You don't?" Theo drank from his glass, licked his upper lip, and set the glass carefully down. "This is weird."

They looked at each other for a minute. Then Miss Stickleback said, "Let's go look for it." Getting up, they walked out of the kitchen and continued through the dining room and the living room—there was a long terrace along both of these rooms facing uptown. They passed a small library room and went down a hall. Along the way, they peeked into the empty bedrooms that also looked uptown onto Seventy-seventh Street. They passed Miss Stickleback's bedroom and then reached the study at the end of the hall.

"We're right at the back of the building here, and as you can see, this is it. There is no terrace. There never has been a terrace. When my great-great-uncle split up this floor, he never mentioned a terrace."

"How strange." Theo held his chin with his left thumb and forefinger. "Let's go check my apartment."

They left Miss Stickleback's apartment, crossed the foyer serving the one elevator that made it this high in the building, and went into Theo's apartment. Again they walked through all the rooms, stopping in the living room to say hello to Theo's mother, who was playing solitaire on the coffee table. Finally they arrived at Theo's parents' large bedroom. There was no terrace to be seen here either. Windows looked out toward the backs of the buildings on Lexington Avenue, but that was it.

"I've an idea," said Miss Stickleback. "Let's do some surveying. Back to the front door. I want to measure this."

They stepped into the foyer next to the elevator again. "This elevator," said Miss Stickleback, "I happen to know, is right in the middle of the building. All right. Here's what I want you to do. I want you to hold the apartment doors open for me. I'm going to pace off your apartment and find out how wide it is. Here we go. One, two, three, four..." Miss Stickleback marched deliberately into Theo's apartment, through the small inside front hall, into the kitchen, and to its south wall. "Eleven, twelve, thirteen, fourteen. Times two makes twenty-eight paces across the front of the building at this height. Now the side walls go straight all the way to the back, at least it does on my side, and I presume on yours too." Theo nodded. "So the back wall should be the same as the front."

Miss Stickleback massaged her delicate chin with both hands. "Now let's measure the back rooms, on your side and on my side. They should add up to twenty-eight."

Miss Stickleback carefully paced off the back of Theo's

apartment, which was his parents' large bedroom. Then they returned to Miss Stickleback's apartment to measure her two back rooms. Theo's parents' bedroom and Miss Stickleback's study and bedroom together had each equaled ten of Miss Stickleback's paces.

Theo said, "Ten times two is twenty. We're missing eight paces."

"Eight paces. Eight missing paces. Could it be the terrace you saw, I wonder?" Miss Stickleback rocked on her heels a little. "Let's make one last test to make sure our math is correct.

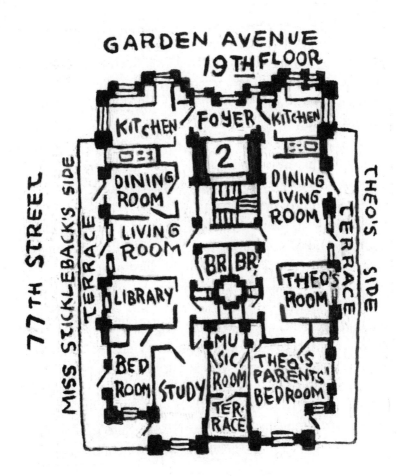

As far as I've always believed, this wall here"—Miss Stickle-back knocked on a wall of her study—"the south wall of my study should be the north wall of your parents' bedroom. Funny I've never ever heard anything through here. At the same time, it's not an outside wall. It never gets cold. Tell you what. You run around to your parents' bedroom and knock three times loud on the wall."

Theo nodded in understanding.

"Then come back here."

A minute and a half later, Theo stood breathing heavily in front of Miss Stickleback.

"Well?" he said, between breaths.

"Nothing," said Miss Stickleback. "Didn't hear a thing. Something mysterious sits between our apartments. Is it the terrace? Might it even be a forgotten room?" Miss Stickleback rubbed her slim hands together. "We must get to the bottom of this. Follow me."

They headed back to the foyer between the apartments. Theo put his head into his own apartment and shouted, "Mom, I'm going downstairs with Miss Stickleback. We're going sleuthing! We're hunting for clues!"

"Okay, dear," came the quiet voice from the living room.

Theo and Miss Stickleback took the elevator to the basement. "Do you think Oskar will be on duty today?" said Theo.

"I think he usually comes in, even on his days off," said Miss Stickleback.

In the basement, they walked along the gray-painted halls until they reached the superintendent's office. They could hear music coming from within. They knocked.

In a moment the door was whisked open with an upswell of music and there in the warm, bright light stood Oskar, large and well-bellied, with a red face, white hair over his ears, and a broad smile, holding a large glass of beer.

"Happy New Year!" he said. "Miss Stickleback. Theo! What took you so long? Theo, have a beer. Miss Stickleback, tea?"

Oskar ushered them into the small windowless room and had them sit on the low, battered, red leather sofa—salvaged from the castoffs of a departing resident long ago—as Marilyn, the building manager's assistant, stood up from it. Mr. Bunchley, sitting on a metal chair next to Oskar's desk, held a glass of white wine and smiled.

Mr. Bunchley, putting down his glass, walked to the back of the office and filled an electric kettle at a small sink, saying over his shoulder, "Perhaps you'd prefer tea as well, Theo?"

"Thanks, Mr. Bunchley," said Theo.

"So, so, so," said Oskar. "What brings you to the basement? Besides the elevator!"

Miss Stickleback sat as straight as she could on the battered sofa.

"You may or may not believe this, Oskar, but we believe that Theo has discovered a forgotten room. There is a missing eight paces!"

"What? That cannot be." Oskar took a large gulp of beer. "Start from the beginning."

Miss Stickleback first told Theo's story and then their story together, while accepting the cup of Earl Grey tea that Mr. Bunchley silently handed her.

"My goodness. Is it possible?"

Getting up, and politely asking Marilyn to step to the right, Oskar pulled open a long, low metal drawer of a flat filing cabinet. He lifted out an enormous—nearly three foot by four foot—book and laid it upon his desk. "Here are the building's original plans," he said. "Now you probably know," he continued, slowly lifting and smoothing over the pages, "your floor was rebuilt in the 1930s. In 1930 to be exact, I believe."

"Yes, my great-great-uncle used to have the entire floor."

"Exactly," said Oskar. "Ah, here we are."

Oskar smoothed out the page marked Floor 19.

"So, as you can see from the plan, here is the elevator. The stairs. You can see a main entry to the apartment doesn't exist no more now it's two apartments. Yours and yours. But you can see where it was."

"Yes, I see," said Miss Stickleback, putting down her tea, and moving to Oskar's side at the desk. "Here's where my living room is, and kitchen. Bedrooms. Library. My study. Yes."

"And here's my apartment," said Theo, at Miss Stickleback's side. "Our living room got put there and the kitchen is here. What's this little X thing?"

"That is the old dumbwaiter. Gone now."

Miss Stickleback and Theo walked their fingers along the floor plans of their own halves of the apartment slowly calling out the names of the rooms they must be passing through. Stopping when they arrived at where the back rooms are now, they turned to look at each other.

"Look," Miss Stickleback exclaimed in her sharp, high voice, tapping a finger loudly on the book. "There's a room!"

Theo, Miss Stickleback, Oskar, Mr. Bunchley, and Marilyn bent their heads close together as they peered over the yellow paper of the large page.

"And a little terrace," said Theo.

"My Gott," said Oskar.

Fifteen minutes later all five of them stood in Miss Stickleback's study, staring at the side wall. The book of plans lay open on her lilac love seat.

"The old door should be behind that," said Oskar, pointing at a large armoire. "We'll have to move it. All right?"

Mr. Bunchley and Oskar heaved, pushed, and cajoled the heavy armoire away from the wall.

As the armoire moved inch by inch like a crotchety old elephant, Theo and Miss Stickleback stood staring at the slowly widening space behind. The armoire had been her mother's and had always stood in just that spot. Even the painters had never moved it. "Just paint around," Miss Stickleback had said, and they always did.

Now the widening yellowy-white rectangle of ancient un-covered wall held everyone spellbound until Theo exclaimed, "There it is!"

The outline of a door showed clearly in the wall where the doorway itself had been walled up in plaster. Though the moldings had been removed, as the building had shifted and fidgeted over the decades, little cracks showed exactly where the doorway had been.

The next morning, the second day of the new year, as the January gray of the New York sky got a little less gray, the forgotten room woke up to the sound of drilling in its north wall. The drilling rattled away at a high pitch. Then a heavier, lower rattle droned and shook the wall becoming slowly louder until with a hiss the end of a large, spinning, silver bit poked through, sending dust and small pieces of plaster onto the floor. The silver bit withdrew. There was a pause. And then there was even louder drilling. Another bit appeared and disappeared. Then the end of a tough red finger emerged and tapped and probed around the edge of the hole.

The finger went away and a watery brown eye appeared. It was replaced by a bright gray-blue one and then a dusty green one.

Some muffled conversation could be heard but not understood through the hole.

Another pause.

Then the sound of a hammer striking hard repeated steadily a dozen times, stopping and then beginning again. After fifteen minutes of this, a piece of wall the size of a framed diploma broke through and fell heavily to the floor, sending bits of itself skidding over to the draped legs of old Mrs. Waterby's piano.

Oskar's face appeared in the hole, along with a "Son of a gun!," then Mrs. Stickleback's face, then Theo's.

Now there was more furious pounding, loud talking, laughter, and more pounding.

Some while later, Oskar, Mrs. Stickleback, and Theo stood by the piano in the center of the forgotten room and slowly looked around. Dust motes floated slowly in the thin morning light.

On the second Saturday of April of that year, around dusk of that early-spring day, the first notes of Chopin's Nocturne no. 6 in G minor sounded, echoing gently between the embracing walls to the north and south before falling lightly into the courtyards below.

Miss Stickleback sat at her great-great-aunt's piano and carefully struck the keys with her elegant fingers and touched the pedals with her feet.

Theo sat between his parents in the first row of chairs on the terrace along with the fifteen other invited neighbors, including Mrs. MacDougal.

Oskar and Mr. Bunchley stood on the other side of the piano near the door to Miss Stickleback's apartment.

In the months since its discovery the forgotten room had

recuperated, Oskar overseeing all the work. Its walls and ceiling had been replastered, new coats of paint in eggshell and high gloss, Naples yellow and bright white had been gently applied. The old Persian rug was cleaned by experts who brought its reds and blacks beautifully back to vigor. The floor was replaced in bamboo, and, of course, the piano was cleaned carefully top to bottom, low to high, and tuned. Miss Stickleback had placed a photograph of her great-great-aunt, showing a graceful young woman, on the piano lid. The terrace was swept and waterproofed, and Mr. Bunchley contributed a potted rosebush, which was placed along the railing. Together Theo and Miss Stickleback carefully washed each glass bead of the small chandelier.

The last chord of Chopin slowly moved into each corner of the room and lingered there until its notes had become a part of the walls themselves. There's not another way to say it— the forgotten room was fully awake once more, its long uncomfortable sleep was over. It was alive again. And it was magical.

Miss Stickleback turned to Beethoven.

Mouse Exchange

SOMETIMES you like a change.

You want to see something new. You grow tired of your same four walls. And you would like to see how other people live.

So you decide to swap houses with someone in a faraway place. You give them your house in exchange for theirs. Just for a month, say.

Now, this sort of thing, while understandable, is frowned upon by building managers—and even more so by someone like Mrs. MacDougal.

"These people coming with their children and their suitcases! I don't know what's in those suitcases!" she said. "How would I? They could be full of bombs for all I know!"

So it's frowned upon and doesn't happen very often. But there is one set of building residents over which the wishes of Mrs. MacDougal have no sway whatsoever—the building's mice.

Mrs. MacDougal can shake her fist all she wants and send off a hundred e-mails to the building manager and the board of directors, the mice of the building run things their own way, and they love a good house exchange.

The Brownbacks, for example, who live at 777 Garden Avenue and are, therefore, city mice, took a different house in the country every summer. However, like any family, the Brownbacks didn't always agree on what made for a vacation and what made for an ordeal.

"This is lovely!" said Mrs. Brownback, emerging from the long entryway into the grand living room of their home for the next month. "So spacious!"

She moved quickly from one corner to the next, pushing her nose into the furnishings, running her quick fingers over everything she came across.

"Oh, look, they've left us some acorns and they're huge!" she said, holding an acorn high above her head. "We are going to eat well here!"

"Mom, I hate acorns," said Jimmy Brownback, her eldest. "Don't they have any pizza, or maybe some Chinese food?"

Jimmy was following his mother into the living room when Mr. Brownback entered, carrying two pieces of luggage, which he dropped loudly onto the straw floor. He gave the place a stern once-over with his large brown eyes. Then addressing his wife he said, "Have you looked at the fields out there? Breathtaking is the word. Breathtaking! I can hardly breathe! There's something weird about the air!" He clawed at his throat.

"It's called fresh air, dear," said Mrs. Brownback. "Trust me, you'll get used to it, and you'll love it. Besides, it's good for your digestion."

"Leave me alone with what's good for my digestion!" said

Mr. Brownback. "I'll decide what's good and what's not good for my digestion!"

Mr. Brownback burrowed into the couch. You must remember, however, that Mr. Brownback's complaints were all part of the fun of the thing.

A moment later, Ernie, Eddie, Edith, Emily, and Frank, the quintuplets, appeared in the living room and began swarming over everything in sight, talking and joking and exclaiming about their discoveries all at once, as was their habit.

On the other hand, sometimes the adventure can be disappointing.

Mr. Brownback pressed the front door keys into Mr. Whitefoot's paw and told him again how to get to the basement, what to do if the toilet backs up, whom to see with any little electrical problems. Then, with a twitch of his delicate tail, he turned to catch up with the rest of the family already headed to the countryside and the Whitefoots' home. The whole Whitefoot clan was eager to explore its new home for a month, sure that it would be the starting place for wonderful new experiences.

The Whitefoots were a family of nine. There were Mr. and Mrs. Whitefoot, and then, in no particular order, since they were all the same age, Jerry, June, Jumper, Jean, Jennifer, Jasmine, and Jack. Their home in the country was beneath an ancient spiny fitzer on the old Cliffdale Farm. It was a kind of garden apartment. It had numberless rooms (arithmetic is not stressed in mouse education) arranged within and around the fitzer's thickest roots, where the Brownback family was no doubt at that moment continuing to exclaim over the spaciousness of the digs.

Mrs. Whitefoot, contrariwise in the Brownbacks' apartment at 777 Garden Avenue, was exclaiming over the cramped quarters she was facing now.

"How do they live like this? I have to tuck in my tail just to turn around!"

The Brownback apartment was, by local standards, a rather swell mousehole, as it occupied much of the interior of the wall that separated Miss Nancy's kitchen from Miss Nancy's living room. The naked hot-water pipe in the wall kept things warm year-round, and where its joint led to the kitchen sink, it provided an excellent surface for warming up leftovers. Also, as the walls were old, the latticework that appeared here and there out of the crumbling plaster provided a wonderful array of beds, stacked up as far as little mouse eyes could see.

And there was very convenient access to Miss Nancy's kitchen. A large hole that let in the gas pipes opened onto the back of the oven. From there it was an easy couple of jumps to get out under and up and into the oven, which Mr. Whitefoot and Jean promptly did, returning half a minute later with cheeks full of goodies.

"Thay," said Mr. Whitefoot, "the landlady here ith a pretty good cook, munch, munch. Here," he continued, removing pawfuls of crisped brown potato bits, crunchy pizza crustlets, and hardened soufflé morsels, and handing them around.

In the meantime, Jumper and Jasmine had found Miss Nancy's bedroom, the clothes dresser, and above all, the sock drawer. This looked softer than any countryside bed of layered straw, milkweed down, and even duck feathers ever could.

And then, after the first snoopings, Mr. and Mrs. Whitefoot were discussing the itinerary for the next days when Jerry, June, and Jennifer burst back into the main mouse living room followed by a panting Jack.

"We saw it! We saw it!" they all shouted at once.

The others stared a bit.

"We saw it!" said Jack.

"What? What did you see?" cried Mrs. Whitefoot.

"The cat!" said Jack.

"Oh!" said Mrs. Whitefoot.

"I knew there would be one here!" said Jack.

"The brochure didn't mention anything about cats," said Mrs. Whitefoot.

Later, when the elder Whitefoots were taking their siesta, Jack said to Jumper, "We saw the cat. And I'm going to fight it!"

Jumper just twitched her whiskers.

At this time, the cat Jack saw, Miss Nancy's cat, Carole Lombard, lay belly-up on the sofa, paws stretched over her head. Quite unaware that the apartment had new tenants, she grunted contentedly in her sleep.

Jack was a bit of a lad. He was a doer, a darer, and a diver-in. Don't let the name "mouse" mislead you. Large as a baby, Jack was huge as an adolescent. He came out last of the litter, but he came out biggest. And even then he came out swinging—his tail, anyway.

Never a bully, mind you, yet always ready to scrap. First, it was playful fisticuffs or sparring with his sisters and brothers. And then he had more serious bouts with other mice in the countryside. Very soon he was noticed at the neighborhood gym in the overturned apple crate next to the barn. From the first afternoon Jack set four feet in the boxing ring of the apple crate, he knew this was home. He was a born fighter.

Henceforth, every afternoon, Jack raced straight from school to the apple crate. He watched the old fighters, learning from them as he did them favors, carrying their gloves, washing their towels, holding the punching bag. Soon enough, however, Jack began training as well. Jumping rope with his tail, shadowboxing, punching the punching bag—his training routine was extremely strenuous. And to fuel his newly rippling muscles, Jack took to eating eight, ten, even eleven entire pumpkin seeds at a time, which is a lot if you're a little mouse.

And this is precisely what Jack no longer was: He was a big mouse, a mammoth mouse, hamster-size at least, maybe even rat-size. And because of his liking for pumpkin seeds—plenty of protein there—he became known as Pumpkinseed Jack.

Pumpkinseed Jack entered the ring formally when he turned nineteen weeks, that is, about the usual age for a young mouse fighter. From his very first fight he broadcast to the neighborhood that he was a mouse to watch. Though he was sometimes prone to leave his nose unprotected—he didn't always keep his paws up—he had a worrying jab and a tremendous left-and-right-hook combination that, by the time he was twenty-two weeks old, had left a string of knocked-out mice in the ring. None had lasted through more than the fourth round.

And when no more mice in the neighborhood would face him, Jack looked farther afield. His fame grew. Mice from all around the countryside came to the apple crate to fight him— and to lose. Jack looked even farther afield. He boxed a vole, a shrew, and a mole in quick order and none could withstand him. The mole, though blind, had a formidable nose that could tell where each of Jack's sweaty paws was at all times, and the mole possessed talented paws of his own that were like steel shovels. The mole landed a couple of blows to Jack's left ear and belly, which, for the first time in his career, surprised Jack. They had sent him reeling for a couple of seconds. Still Jack pulled himself together, danced forward and back as the mole lumbered heavily, then polished the mole off with an extended flurry of combination punches, the likes of which that sporting crowd at the apple crate had never ever seen before.

As a matter of fact, the mole only whetted Jack's appetite for ever more challenging opponents. In the weeks that followed, Jack took on a rat (mean and ruthless), a squirrel (squirrely), and a muskrat (big, but slow and stupid). Jack defeated them all. Then he dispatched a chipmunk, a flying squirrel, and an enormous gopher. Jack was the greatest fighting mouse anyone had ever seen.

When Mrs. Whitefoot had announced her intention that the family would spend a month in the city, Jack couldn't believe his good luck. This would be a chance for him to make his mark in the wider world. New York City! Where Muhammad Ali had fought! Where Mike Tyson was born! Where Knut Knuckleson, the Norwegian Rat from Sheepshead Bay, got his start!

As Jack had dispatched one local fighter after another, his fame grew. He became the hero of little mice from yards around. But Jack had begun to crave more. He wanted to face the toughest opponent. He wanted to fight on the biggest stage. It was his dream to fight a cat in New York City. If he could win that one, his name would go up in lights with all the rest. It would be the Fight of the Century.

And now here was his chance. Everything had lined up as he'd hoped. He had the city. He had the cat. Now he needed the fight.

While Jack planned the Fight of the Century, the rest of the Whitefoot clan threw itself into seeing all that the city had to offer. They took in spectacular shows. Not on Broadway exactly; the shows were on Miss Nancy's enormous flat-screen

TV in the living room. Nevertheless the programs astounded all the Whitefoots. Mrs. Whitefoot frequently had to shush her brood to keep their squeals of astonishment from betraying the location of the prime seats they had inside the radiator cover. Also, they ate out nearly every night—sometimes in Miss Nancy's oven, other times higher up in the kitchen cabinets where the Rice Krispies and Kashi Medley tasted even better than ever because of the fabulous view they had from there. Evenings, if they weren't watching the big screen, the Whitefoots might venture outside their immediate nest, into the walls of other apartments on their own floor or the floors above and below.

This is what they really liked. Just watching the great parade of city life—mice, cockroaches, and even a rat or two—was the very best entertainment. Everything was moving about, scuttling and scurrying. It was like an endless party. The Whitefoots always came home from these excursions utterly exhausted, tumbling into bed and sleeping through the day. They became only truly awake again when the nighttime returned.

While the rest of the family saw shows, ate fine foods, and strolled like boulevardiers, Jack trained. And he studied his opponent. After the first excitement of seeing the cat, Jack had settled down to a more systematic observation. The cat was a female—mice can sense these things—not in great shape, but big. At least once a day the human being in the house, Miss Nancy, hitched the cat up to some kind of leather device and left the apartment with the cat. Jack wasn't sure exactly what the meaning of this was but assumed it was some kind of fitness training. The cat had twice-a-day meals and nibbled in between. She had good-size paws, plenty of teeth, fine white whiskers. All in all, she looked like a worthy and truly formidable opponent.

That evening, as Jack jumped his tail the usual thousand times, he pondered his fight strategy. The cat's paws were large. No doubt about that. He would have to be quick enough to avoid a direct blow anywhere. Even Jack knew that he couldn't survive too many punches a cat like that could give him. He would have to get in close, lead with his snappy left jab and then rely on a barrage of hooks. In fact, Jack reasoned, if he got in close enough quickly enough he could neutralize the danger from the cat paws, because if the cat tried to really punch him, she would wind up punching herself instead. He would just need to get inside those paws right away and then stay inside them. Of course, that would bring him closer to the cat's mouth. He wasn't sure what rules the cat would be playing by. She might just call "home rules" and try to bite his head off.

He would have to be ready for that.

Jack talked to his sisters, Jumper and Jean. He asked Jean to be his manager and Jumper to be his promoter. Jean had managed Jack on a couple of previous occasions and she had been quite helpful—her insights were good. When the mole clobbered Jack in round two of their fight, it was Jean who had helped him recover. She told Jack to move his feet quickly and then go for a crippling flurry of punches. It had been a gamble, but it had worked. Jack said to Jean, "I want to have your eyes in my corner."

Jumper, too, had worked with Jack before. When Jack had worried that the nickname "Pumpkinseed" made him look weak, Jumper said the opposite. "Use it," she said. "Own it. It's colorful. It's unusual. It stands out." With a winning streak of fifteen knockouts and counting, if any mouse had ever thought Pumpkinseed Jack was wimpy, they didn't anymore.

So while Jean and Jack settled into their twice-daily training sessions, Jumper started to shape the publicity campaign. The first decision to be made was this: Did they want to inform the cat that she would be on the receiving end of a mouse fight? On the one hand, letting the cat know where and when the fight was going to take place would make sure she was prepared and present for the occasion. On the other hand the cat might invite friends—other cats—to the fight, and this could put a real damper on the resident mouse turnout. Your average mouse stays pretty far away from a room full of cats. Even if they were upstanding sports fans, they were cats, after all. That was the whole glamour of the fight. Still, one cat was enough. So in the end, the three decided to keep the great cat-mouse fight a secret from the cat.

"Remember, we're going to have to go in hard early, like with the mole," said Jean, "but this time even harder and earlier. Your feet have to be moving like whirligig beetles in a cup of hot coffee, and your paws should be a buzzing blur!"

Jack continued to shadowbox as Jean coached him, grunting little mouse grunts as he swung his fists.

Jumper deputized Jerry and Jennifer to make the posters. Jerry wrote the copy—the words—Jennifer did the design, and between two and three in the morning, they managed to print fifty-seven copies, which was all the paper that was in the paper feed on Miss Nancy's printer.

That night while she worked on the poster, Jumper had examined the walls of Miss Nancy's study.

"Wow, look at these fabulous Broadway posters!" said Jumper. Jumper couldn't have known it, but Nancy was herself a Broadway publicist.

"Forget Broadway," said Jerry. "Look at this instead," and he rolled out the eight-and-a-half-inch by eleven-inch, two-mouse-tall poster.

Jumper read the poster.

THE FIGHT OF THE CENTURY!

Jack "Pumpkinseed" Whitefoot vs. the Cat in apartment
11B. Weighing in at a hefty eight and a half ounces, Jack
comes into the match at fifteen and zero, all knockouts,
to challenge the cat, weighing who knows how much
with who knows how many wins. One thing we do
know is she's a cat. And this is the first mouse-cat fight
in history. The World Mouse Boxing Federation wouldn't
sanction this fight. They said it was too dangerous, but
we're bringing it to you anyway!

Be in the living room at midnight, August 11th, for
the event of da century!

After the poster went up, hung in various nooks and crannies,
the usual low hubbub within the walls of 777 Garden Avenue
was a high hubbub, as mice, rats, and cockroaches from every
floor got an eyeful of the poster.

"What's up?" said the mouse from 11A.

"Some kid from the sticks is trying to make a name for
himself. Wants to fight the cat in 11B."

"Cheese!"

"He may not get what he's looking for!"

"You said it."

As in the above conversation, the reaction among the locals
was mixed. Still, everyone was curious, everyone was talking
about it, and certainly everyone planned to show up for the
fight.

It was inevitable that eventually Mrs. Whitefoot would
hear of it as well.

"Pumpkinseed Jack to fight the cat in apartment 11B,"
she squeaked. "Jack! Where is that boy? When I get through
with him, he really will have lived through the fight of the
century. Oh!"

"Now, honey," said Mr. Whitefoot, "don't be too hard on him. This means a lot to him."

"It'll mean a lot to me if he gets himself eaten!"

The ensuing family, er, discussion lasted till the gray dawn rising outside the kitchen window sent the family scurrying out from behind the toaster, where they had been arguing about the situation. Jumper, Jean, Jerry, and Jennifer had come in for a good bit of criticism from Mrs. Whitefoot as well for being aiders and abettors.

While Mr. Whitefoot tried to stay neutral—though, undeniably, he had a soft spot for Jack—June and Jasmine took their mother's part.

However, badger, stamp her delicate white feet, and even howl as she did, Mrs. Whitefoot could not sway Jack from his determination to go through with the fight. Mr. Whitefoot, who secretly was looking forward to the fight and even had bet a few pieces of Muenster cheese on it, did his best to console his wife, saying that even if Jack was eaten there was always next summer's litter to look forward to.

At last the sun went down on the Saturday of the fight. All day long various mice had kept an eye on Carole Lombard, looking for any signs that she knew the fight was approaching or that she was off her food or in any way behaving oddly. All reports indicated that Carole Lombard was having a usual day and that she was in tip-top form. She'd had a good breakfast at seven. She had napped in various chairs and on Miss Nancy's bed till noon. She had nibbled dry food and lapped water. At two fifteen she had gone out for her training run. Had dined again at five. She had stretched. She had cleaned her claws. She had gnawed on her feet. Ominously, she had occasionally run her rough tongue over her cruel teeth, teeth that no rodent possessed, a carnivore's teeth. As the watchers reported to an eager public in the walls, the cat in apartment

11B was ugly and extremely dangerous. If tonight was like every other night, she would be dozing on the living-room sofa when the kitchen clock struck midnight.

Jack had spent the day in a careful last preparation. He followed Jean's thoughtful program exactly. He, too, napped in the morning and again in the afternoon. His workout was gentle. At five, Jean gave him a complete rubdown.

Meanwhile, Mrs. Whitefoot made one last attempt to get the fight called off.

"Mr. Whitefoot," she pleaded, "do something. There's no way Jack can survive this fight! It's never happened! Mice run from cats. That's the way it's been for a million million years. If you let Jack go through with this, it will be the end of him. Don't you see?"

Mr. Whitefoot just patted his wife's back and gently nuzzled her whiskers.

The rest of the evening was quiet. Miss Nancy made herself a bacon, lettuce, and tomato sandwich on rye, watched a little television, and then went to bed. When Miss Nancy let the mystery novel fall shut and turned off the light, Carole Lombard wandered to the living room and found her favorite corner of the sofa.

It was eleven twenty.

Half an hour later, Jack Pumpkinseed Whitefoot stepped out onto the living-room carpet—a lovely Persian one in reds and grays. It was ten minutes to midnight. Ten minutes to the Fight of the Century. All around him, behind the radiator, under the sofa, behind the cracked baseboard, hundreds of mice, a thousand cockroaches, and two interested rats waited quietly. Jack stretched his back legs one after the other, rolled his neck first clockwise and then counterclockwise. He shadowboxed silently but in a sprightly way.

At two minutes to midnight, the crowd edged forward.

At last the kitchen clock began to strike the hour. At the tenth stroke the multitude of four- and six-footed city folk surged out from their hiding places, forming a ring around the Persian rug. There was an odd smallish rumbling, the sound of the excited buzz in the rodent and insect household.

With the last stroke of midnight a hush fell over the living room. Only the hum of the refrigerator and the gentle wheezing of the sleeping cat could be heard.

Jack drew himself up and squeaked with a mighty voice, "Hello! Miss cat! Wake up! You are in for the Fight of the Century!"

Carole Lombard woke up with a start. She lifted her head and looked left and right, instantly fully awake. Her hairs stood out. Her whiskers twitched. Her eyes narrowed. She got up, arched her back quickly, and took two steps to the edge of the sofa, from which she looked down at the carpet.

Her eyes locked onto the lone mouse standing on his hind legs in the center of the carpet. Her eyes narrowed to slits. Her whiskers twitched ferociously. Everything about Carole Lombard said that she could not believe what she was seeing.

And then she believed it. With a shriek that woke up the nine-year-old boy sleeping in the apartment below, Carole Lombard leaped from the sofa, over the head of Jack and all the assembled public, and then shot like an exploded furry balloon down the apartment hall. After a half second of frantic clawing at the door into Miss Nancy's bedroom, she darted in, and with a practiced jump, she landed on the top of Miss Nancy's armoire, where she crouched, hiding as well as she could behind a small vinyl suitcase. She was shivering like a blade of grass in a piping breeze.

The truth of the matter is, as with so many of her city sisters and brothers, Carole Lombard was frightened to death of mice.

It was a bedraggled, disgruntled, and thoroughly disappointed Whitefoot family that greeted the Brownbacks a week later, who were returning to their apartment inside the walls of 777 Garden Avenue after their six weeks in the country.

Only Mrs. Whitefoot spoke when Mrs. Brownback asked them how their time had been.

"It was wonderful!" she said. "The shows! The food! And all the interesting people! I don't know how you get any sleep here with all the excitement! However it's time for us to get back home."

Once home, Pumpkinseed Jack hung up his boxing gloves. The whole episode kind of unnerved him, as a trip to the city so often does to country mice.

He stopped in for a ginger ale with the mole one afternoon.

"You couldn't drag me to the city," said the mole. "Even though I hear they have a lot of nice tunnels."

"Why not?" said Jack.

"Too dangerous!"

Jack grunted and thoughtfully sipped his ginger ale.

OTIS

MRS. MACDOUGAL and the building manager sat opposite each other in the building manager's office, he behind a large desk covered in papers and phones, and she in a vinyl-covered armchair, where she absentmindedly let the pages of a magazine, Today's Bricks, fall slowly from back to front.

"Elevator Number Two is very old," she said.

"It is very old," he said, not looking up from the financial report he was reading.

"The light is dim. The metal is scratched in places. The wood paneling is somewhat discolored. And the marble in the floor is badly cracked. Shoddy. Second-rate. Not modern. With visitors to the building, who may be of some importance..."

"... some importance," he said.

"... this makes for a bad impression."

"... bad impression..."

"What's more," continued Mrs. MacDougal, "Elevator Number Two seems to be possessed by a demon. I have on more than one occasion been deposited on the wrong floor.

Or taken up when I pushed Down. Or held between floors for minutes at a time. It felt like hours. Horrible!"

"…horrible…" he said.

"It is fortunate that I live on the fifteenth floor and so may take Elevators Number One and Three as an alternative to Elevator Number Two. But some of those unfortunate enough to live above me must take Elevator Number Two, since it is, as you know, the only one that reaches the highest parts of the building."

"…highest parts…"

"So it is almost painfully clear that we must rip out Elevator Number Two and replace it with something new. Something nice. Modern. With some elegant details."

For the first time the building manager looked up from his papers. He said, "Rip out Elevator Number Two? Rip out? Elevator Number Two? Mrs. Rotterdam-Bottom's never going to agree to that. Oh no. You can put that thought right out of your mind. Mrs. Rotterdam-Bottom has a thing for Elevator Number Two. She won't budge on that." He closed the report. "Do you want to know why?"

It was this way.

Mrs. Rotterdam-Bottom is nearly ninety years old and so is Elevator Number Two. It is sometimes called simply "Otis" by the residents because that name, the name of the manufacturer, stares up from a wrought-iron disk in the otherwise cracked, as Mrs. MacDougal pointed out, marble floor. Before her marriage, Mrs. Rotterdam-Bottom was simply Miss Rotterdam. She and Otis were installed in the building at almost the same time. Old Mr. Rotterdam, Miss Rotterdam's grandfather, had the original elevator replaced with the new Otis just before Miss Rotterdam was born. Though the original eleva-

tor had shown no signs of age or debility, old Mr. Rotterdam
wanted the newest and the best for his first grandchild. What's
more, the new Otis was one of the very first fully automatic
elevators installed in the city. Being fully automatic, Otis
eliminated the need for old Mr. Rotterdam to pay an elevator
operator's salary, which old Mr. Rotterdam quietly liked a lot.

Otis arrived with a load capacity of two thousand pounds,
a thirty-horsepower motor, and could do the trip from the
basement to the twenty-first floor in two minutes and eight
seconds. Installing Otis had gone smoothly. It took six weeks,
but there were no complications.

Likewise with little Miss Rotterdam, only in her case it required six hours and not six weeks to be born.

Miss Rotterdam arrived weighing eight pounds, nine
ounces. She had a tremendous appetite and lots of vim.

Otis carried Mrs. Rotterdam, old Mr. Rotterdam's daughter-
in-law, to the lobby on her way to the hospital maternity
ward, and took her with her new baby, Delphinia Rotterdam,
up from the lobby, home to the twentieth floor.

Everyone was well pleased.

Nearly coincidentally, that is, about one week later, Otis
performed a very similar service for Mr. and Mrs. Bottom,
who lived in apartment 7C. Alexander Bottom, a healthy nine
pounds, four ounces, with an even bigger appetite than Delphinia's, came to 777 Garden Avenue to take up his position
as chief joy of the Bottom family, where he was known as
Sandy.

In a way, Otis, Delphinia, and Sandy made up that year's
freshman class at 777.

The three soon found their voices, their legs, and their call
buttons.

Right away, Delphinia announced her literary ambitions to
the world by gnawing on one book after another. She could

read by the time she was three and had a good chunk of Dickens under her belt by the time she was eight. She began to write occasional pieces for The Gardenia, our magazine of avenue news, illustrated with photos from the camera Delphinia, now known as Phinny, received from her mother on her ninth birthday.

Sandy, also an early gnawer, differed from Delphinia in that, even at ages three, four, and five, he continued to gnaw, though by five it was no longer so much on non-food items. His gnawing became more refined: corn on the cob, chicken legs, apple pies. By the time he was eight, Sandy could distinguish Jonagold from Mutsu from Red Delicious in a blind taste test of apples fresh from the market.

And Otis? Being an elevator, he matured much more rapidly. There were some misunderstandings in the first few weeks of his life, Otis not being able to distinguish between nine and six, for instance (they do look alike). Also, sometimes he got tired, especially in the late afternoon–early evening, when he was almost constantly on the go. Now and then he took a breather between floors, especially if he was at or near his weight capacity—about seven people. The shouting and hullabaloo this brought on, though, would give him such a headache that he might shut down for the rest of the evening, making everyone have to take Elevator Number One and Elevator Number Three, and then the stairs from floors seventeen to twenty.

But after a few house calls by the elevator specialists, all of these minor complaints were corrected.

By the time he was two years old, Otis was in peak form and running like a top.

And he was beginning to develop a personality. Every once in a while, he liked his little jokes. He might close his door halfway and then open it again, and then close it, which can kind of make any rider think he or she was in a little time warp. Or Otis would slow down or speed up, especially if he had a nice long stretch to do, say from the first floor to the twentieth. Or if a lady was carrying a lot of packages he might close his door on her gently and hold her for a mere second or two, just for a lark.

Occasionally, of course, like anyone else, he got angry. He hated dogs piddling in him. Yuck! Or when someone punched his buttons. Punched his buttons! "Punch nine for me, please." Really! Who likes being punched? Bouncing a ball, farting, smoking, talking too loud, all got on his nerves. He never held anyone between floors to take his revenge—keeping whoever was so annoying a second longer inside him was the last thing he wanted. However he did scold in his own way. For instance, he might open and shut his door loudly and repeatedly on the floor of any obnoxious resident, sometimes at four in the morning, if he thought it might teach the offender a lesson.

Still, that was rare. For the most part, Otis was a happy and well-adjusted elevator.

By the time Otis was eight, he was a master elevator, one of the finest in the city and a source of some pride to 777 residents. Remember, this was a long time ago and an automatic elevator was already something pretty special. Naturally he knew every resident by name, most of their guests, and, apart from his rare moments of fun, he served them well.

Now it happens in a building like 777 Garden Avenue that, while an elevator knows all its residents and all the residents know their elevator, not all the residents know all the other residents. So it was with Delphinia and Sandy. That is, they knew each other by sight, had seen each other in the building, of course. But they had never spoken.

In those days the idea of high and low society still mattered, much as we might object to this now. Often, whether you were high or low was indicated by where you lived in the building: high society on the high floors, low society on the low floors.

So it was with Delphinia and Sandy. Delphinia's father, the son of old Mr. Rotterdam, the owner of the building, owned other buildings himself. Delphinia's mother gave and attended parties. Mr. Bottom worked for the city as an accountant. Mrs. Bottom taught English in a high school in Brooklyn. The two families were not necessarily high and low, perhaps, but let's say high and middle; two slices of New York society that didn't much mix.

The same held true for Delphinia's and Sandy's schooling. Delphinia attended the Mockingbird School for Girls. Sandy was a proud student of P.S. 158 around the corner. Different paths to school, different friends, different clothes.

None of this mattered to Otis, however. Otis was an elevator and saw the world as an elevator does, that is, without prejudice, and he saw no reason that the two, Delphinia and Sandy, shouldn't meet and become friends.

Sandy, the youthful gnawer of note, had in his tenth year turned to cooking and was becoming known, especially on his floor, for the wonderful things he baked after school. He was not afraid to experiment, and like every good artist sought an audience with which to share his work and from which to gain criticism or encouragement. On any given afternoon, usually around four thirty, the door to apartment 7C opened, and out would float alluring aromas with Sandy not far behind, holding a tray of, perhaps, hazelnut cookies or fruit bread. He generally had only to let the wonderful smells do his advertising work for him, to bring out one or two taste testers from the neighboring apartments.

Otis was well aware of this routine. So it happened that on a rainy and cold October afternoon, Sandy, waiting for someone to open his or her apartment door and try his oatmeal snickerdoodles, saw instead the elevator door open, revealing a wet, green-clad schoolgirl, who looked hungry—Delphinia. Delphinia, on her part, expecting to step onto the twentieth floor, the penthouse floor, the floor whose button she had pushed, instead saw a boy holding a tray of snickerdoodles.

Delphinia stepped off the elevator.

Sandy stepped toward the elevator.

"Try a snickerdoodle?" said Sandy.

Delphinia, shaking the wet raincoat hood off her head, took a snickerdoodle.

"Thanks, mmph," she said, with a snickerdoodle, more crumbly than she expected, half in her mouth.

"What do you think? It's my first time. Cooking snicker-doodles."

"Delicious. You're very good. At snickerdoodles."

"My name's Alexander. My family calls me Sandy. You live in the penthouse, right?"

"Yes, I'm Delphinia—Phinny."

"You want some hot chocolate? The snickerdoodles, I think, are a little dry and could use some."

Otis, who was standing motionless with his door open, in case Phinny had not liked Sandy's snickerdoodles, closed his door quietly and returned to the lobby.

The afternoon of the snickerdoodles marked the beginning of Sandy and Phinny's friendship, which grew naturally and simply over the next years.

Remember, this was still a long time ago—almost eighty years.

By the time they were in high school—Phinny still at Mock-ingbird and Sandy at Cornelius Van Mooswyck High—they had taken to monthly roams in search of dishes for Sandy to study and other avenues for Phinny to write about, traveling in their quests to every corner of the city: to Queens for schnitzel on Myrtle Avenue, to the Bronx for spaghetti bolognese on Arthur Avenue, to Brooklyn for pierogis on Greenpoint Avenue, to Staten Island for oysters on Castleton Avenue, and in Manhattan for pizza on Mulberry Street and dumplings on Mott.

Often Phinny would find notes from Sandy slipped into her family's mailbox in the building's mail room, which said things like "They've discovered a new kind of chicken with sweet potatoes on Lenox!!! Let's go!! Can you!? Will you?! I've got to try it!!!!" Or "Something mysterious is happening in the risottos on Second Avenue—I think we should check it out!?!" Or even, in a more somber mood, "I'm bored. How 'bout hot dogs on Surf Avenue on Sunday?"

Not unnaturally, Phinny's parents, who shared this mailbox, were curious about Sandy and, after a year of watching the notes come and go, asked Phinny to introduce her to them, as they had assumed that Sandy was a school chum—a girl, in other words.

Phinny didn't bother to clear up that misunderstanding. Both she and Sandy knew by instinct that none of their parents would be keen on them traveling around the city together as far and wide as they did. The Bottoms would not object out of any social misgivings, nevertheless they feared that someday Sandy's feelings might be hurt. Let's be frank, it was the Rotterdams that Phinny and Sandy had to worry about. Mr. Rotterdam, in particular, would most decidedly not approve. Does it need to be spelled out? Mr. Rotterdam might like Sandy personally very much, he might like his jokes and his good taste in food, but he didn't want to see his daughter spending so much time with him with the possible result, some years down the road, she might end up Mrs. Delphinia Rotterdam-Bottom!

Phinny and Sandy understood this. And so, without either making a big deal of it, they carefully avoided Mr. Rotterdam altogether.

As high school wore on, they found that this was not too difficult to do, because they barely found time to see each other, and their trips to far distant avenues were few. Also, the war had begun, World War II, that is, and while their city was never under the duress that so much of the rest of the world endured, life was dark, a little down, and they both liked to stay close to home.

The last high-school trip they did manage was a glorious one to Twenty-third Avenue in Astoria, Queens, for Greek salads and clams. It took place on a sparkling Columbus Day in the fall of their senior year. Phinny had suggested they ride their bicycles, and Sandy had—somewhat reluctantly—agreed. Crossing first the Harlem River to Randall's and Wards Islands, then the East River at Hell Gate, where they rode high over the city on the Triborough Bridge, a feeling of equal joy and terror came over both of them as they looked far down into the churning waters beneath them and then south to the towers of Manhattan. They were giddy at the simple fact that this was where they lived, this was what their neighbors before them had made.

And soon after, joy and terror were replaced by relief and contentment at the scrumptiousness of their neighborly meal.

But that was their only trip of the year.

Phinny had been seeing quite a lot of Styne Van Steen, a senior at Horace Mann School, whom her parents were very excited about (he was the son of very old family friends).

It was Styne Van Steen who was Phinny's date to the big Mockingbird School Spring Ball, but it was Sandy whom Phinny thought about, having left Styne dumbly in the decorated gymnasium, as she walked home down Garden Avenue, thinking that she could go for some good scrambled eggs and waffles.

And there was Sandy walking uptown on Garden Avenue, just coming back from a movie.

They met in front of their building and Sandy said, "How about some scrambled eggs and waffles? There's a new place on Lexington."

The sparkle in Phinny's eyes when she said "Yes" was clear to anyone watching, even from inside the lobby through the glass doors.

Later that night, Otis opened his door for them on the penthouse floor. Sandy had never been that high before, and hesitated on the threshold of the elevator, and so did Phinny. They stood transfixed, looking into each other's eyes, half in and half out of the elevator. Well, if you stand half in and half out of an elevator, holding the door open too long, you know what happens—an alarm goes off. In Otis's case, it was a sharp ringing. This so startled both Sandy and Phinny that they leaped back into the elevator and into each other's arms.

Otis immediately began to descend—all the way to the basement—and then began the return, stopping at no other floors. How it happened that Otis suddenly headed down to the basement and back is anyone's guess. Did Sandy or Phinny lean against the button unwittingly? Who knows? Certainly not Sandy and Phinny, who knew only the thrill their closeness gave them. Otis just started going down. The full round trip takes, without stops, exactly four minutes and thirty-six seconds (twenty seconds for the door to open and close). Four minutes and thirty-six seconds is plenty of time for one careful first kiss, and then two, three, or even four second kisses that aren't careful at all. Four minutes and thirty-six seconds is also plenty of time to fall head over heels, top to bottom, in love.

Well, in love or not, soon after this, both of them went to college. Sandy traveled to New Orleans and the university there to study history and Southern cooking, and Phinny to Boston and the college there to study journalism and art, both departures leaving Otis missing their cheery faces, their sensitive hands, their hummed tunes!

Some loves cool when the parties in question are separated by a thousand or so miles for months at a time. Not this one. They wrote several letters a week and sometimes spoke on the phone, though this was kind of a big deal at the time. They also sent each other things; on Sandy's part historic recipes he had discovered or new ones he concocted himself, and on Phinny's part articles she had written and photographs of paintings she had seen.

Where would it end, this secret romance?

We'll see.

For there was one big fly in their otherwise creamy ointment.

If Phinny had a flaw it was that she couldn't stand up to her father. She could browbeat the toughest student union campaigner to get a good quote for a story; she could endure the bombast of a hoary professor at very close range; she could silence a boozy fraternity classmate with one well-crafted zinger—but she couldn't stand up to her father.

So when her father suggested Styne Van Steen's name to her as the perfect husband whom he expected her to marry upon her college graduation, she didn't say no.

Can you believe it? She didn't say no. True, she never exactly said yes. But she definitely didn't say no. The wedding was to be held on the Rotterdams' spacious northern terrace, nicely shaded from the early-summer sun—a June wedding.

Whether it was to be a June wedding because Mr. Rotterdam happened to hear that Sandy was working at a four-star restaurant in Buenos Aires is a matter of debate, but it would indicate that Mr. Rotterdam had wised up a bit since Phinny was a teenager.

After Phinny didn't say no, she forgot about the whole thing as well as she could. All that spring, Phinny threw herself into her studies and firmly didn't think about Styne Van Steen. In Boston, as she wrote her papers, she didn't think about Styne Van Steen; as she took her photographs, she didn't think about Styne Van Steen; and as she ran around the city with her friends, she didn't think about Styne Van Steen.

But then on the weekends, when she came down to New York by train, Styne Van Steen was there and it was as if she were in a dream. As if in a dream, she chose the stationery that the wedding announcements went out on. Like a sleepwalker, she moved from wedding-dress fitting to fitting. When Styne Van Steen presented her with an enormous engagement ring over dinner, she had looked like a koala bear, large-eyed and silently munching on a leaf. But apparently she didn't comprehend what was going on around her or even right in front of her. She was in a dream. A fog. A terrible haze.

Not so her father, Mr. Rotterdam. He steamed ahead, determined to have his daughter married to a suitable husband as soon as it was possible.

And sure enough, Phinny graduated (with high honors) from her college and then returned to 777 Garden Avenue and the dream of her marriage and she stayed in that dream all the way to the altar, which was set up at the end of the terrace where the birdbath usually stood.

But fortune smiled on Phinny, for when the minister said, "If there is anyone here who carries in him an objection to this union between Delphinia and Styne, let him now speak or forever hold his peace," a voice from somewhere near the back had shouted, "Scrambled eggs and waffles!"

It was enough to break the spell. Phinny blinked a few times. She looked with eyes filled with horror at seeing Styne Van Steen standing a foot to her left. And that look of horror only grew as she shortly took in the minister, the altar, and the gathered audience. All she could do was run, as well as she could in her fancy shoes, in the direction of Sandy's voice.

How Sandy came to be there at all was like this. Sandy arrived home early the night before, his apprenticeship having come to a premature end due to—through no fault of his own—a deadly mayonnaise. Mr. Hilleboe, the head doorman at that time, taking Sandy's small suitcase, rode up with Sandy to the seventh floor in Otis and gave Sandy a complete report, beginning at floor one and ending at floor seven, on what was happening, or about to happen, with Phinny on the penthouse floor.

What was now really happening about and around Phinny on the day of her wedding was near total chaos and mayhem. Mr. Rotterdam was shouting. Phinny kept running. Mrs. Rotterdam was crying. Styne Van Steen was staring with his mouth agape.

Sandy grabbed Phinny's hand and Phinny, who had at last kicked off her high heels, ran with Sandy through the crowded apartment to the front hall and Otis, Sandy practically diving for the elevator call button.

But then a funny thing happened. Though Otis was there, on the penthouse floor, the door didn't open. Sandy and Phinny looked at the floor indicator above the elevator, which told them that Otis was there. Still the door didn't open.

They stared at each other for a couple of ticking seconds, but then, as the noise of pursuing family members and perhaps a fiancé coming to his outraged senses grew louder from within the apartment, Phinny said, "The stairs!"

Now she ran ahead of Sandy, pulling him behind her along

a passageway around Otis and through swinging doors lead-ing to a tight stairwell. Down they plunged, seven steps, four steps, and another seven steps to the next landing. Seven steps, four steps, seven steps to the next landing. At the fifteenth floor, Sandy said, "Stop! Listen!" The stairs ran next to Otis's elevator shaft. They stood in the middle of the top seven steps. Sandy put his ear to the wall.

"Otis's doors just opened." He was quiet. "He's moving! Come on!"

They ran again, now taking the steps two at a time.

"How could Otis do this to us!" shouted Phinny. "He's betrayed us!"

They ran and in spite of the loud slapping feet—Phinny's bare soles, Sandy's brown loafers—they could clearly hear the slight grating of Otis's cables.

At the eleventh floor Phinny said, "Oh my goodness! I have to stop a minute," and she sat down heavily at the top of the four-step turn. Sandy stood above her, leaning on the banister.

They looked at each other and then at the stairway wall. The cables creaked. And then they could hear the muffled voices of the passengers inside as Otis drew nearer. It was about to pass them when the creaking of the cables suddenly stopped.

There was a momentary silence from within.

Then Styne Van Steen's voice was heard, saying, "Hey, we've stopped?"

"Young man, that is rather obvious, I should think," said Phinny's father's voice.

"Punch the buttons! Punch the buttons! Punch them! Punch the buttons!" said Styne.

"Young man..."

Then the sound of, presumably, Styne, banging on Otis's insides, punching buttons, kicking doors.

Next a very eerie silence fell all around them; it was the silence of a noble elevator who will not be moved.

"I don't like this!" shouted Styne. "I think I can't breathe! I'm having one of my attacks! Aaaaaaaaaaaaaaaaaaaaaa!"

"Let's go," said Sandy, quietly.

Phinny started to walk down again, glancing up briefly to say, "My poor father." And then with calm determination they got away down the remaining ten flights of stairs, through the lobby, and into the taxicab that Mr. Hilleboe hailed for them.

Thus began their life together. For the next twenty years, Sandy and Phinny roamed the world in search of interesting food to eat and fascinating avenues to walk, and both to be written about, photographed, and turned into articles and stories that were sent home to be published in sundry magazines. In those days, the hot stories were cabled not e-mailed, the cool stories were airmailed not saved to a cloud. They were dispatched from telegraph and post offices from all of the oddest of the earth's corners.

On the way to one of these offices, some say it was in Rio de Janeiro, and some say it was Kankakee, Illinois, they stopped at the local magistrate's office and were married.

They boarded streetcars on Zinkensdamm in Stockholm to eat boiled eels and potatoes, they came out of the subway at Moctezuma in Mexico City to eat burritos made with ancient maize tortillas, they hailed taxicabs in Singapore to take them to Clarke Quay to eat pepper crab in tamarind sauce.

Naturally, they traveled to Garden Avenue now and then. After several years, when Sandy and Phinny's articles had made them both literary stars in New York and respected journalists the world over, Mr. Rotterdam forgave them both for having run off together so abruptly and turning his world upside down. He even allowed Sandy to cook him dinners from time to time. Mr. and Mrs. Bottom were a bit perplexed by Sandy's good fortune, missed him terribly when he was away, but beamed with pride when they saw his byline at the top of a column of text, sometimes even on page one. Mrs. Rotterdam, too, thrilled at the sight of "D. Rotterdam" beneath a photograph, or "D. Rotterdam" running boldly with "by" above a fascinating traveler's tale.

Even Styne Van Steen was not unhappy, as he had, the very next June, been able to marry the daughter of the owner of 740 Park Avenue, which was, after all, a better address.

When they were at 777, they rested. But after a month or two of sleeping in late, taking steam baths, and watching television in the evenings, a little something began to itch in the backs of their brains, and Sandy and Phinny were once again ready to go. Sandy inevitably would have found some hitherto unnoticed reference to far-flung foods and locales as he prowled the back stacks of quiet libraries.

"Wouldn't you like to stay at home with us for a bit? Do a little decorating? Make some of those great home-cooked meals of yours?" pleaded Mr. Rotterdam. "I could give you a building of your very own. How about it?"

"No, thanks, Dad," Phinny always said. "We still haven't eaten and seen enough of the world." So you see, along with being fearless when it came to crossing international borders, she was no longer afraid of her father, even unafraid of hurting his feelings, which was what her trouble always had been. Perhaps to soften her refusal, she always added, "But we'll settle down someday. I promise."

In their twentieth summer together, Sandy and Phinny found themselves in Rangoon, in Burma, with not much to do. They had each just posted a packet of stories and pictures to New York. And now the problem was what to do next.

Sandy spent his afternoons in the Rangoon library. Then one day he came back to their hotel room to say, "I've found it!"

"What have you found, dear?" said Phinny, looking up from the writing desk.

"The most exotic food in the world! Listen to this." Sandy began to read from a small book, bound in leather.

"'As Mount Everest is to the mountaineer, as the North Pole is to the Arctic trekker, as the Mariana Trench is to the bathysphere diver, so is the Angel's Welcome to the culinary explorer. The Angel's Welcome—as it is known to the monks who prepare it—can only be found at one ancient monastery standing deep in a tropical forest between the toes of the foothills of the Himalayas, and is the rarest, most elusive, and most dangerous food in the world.'" Sandy looked up at Phinny for a moment with large eyes and a spreading smile before he continued reading. "'The Angel's Welcome is a dish made of the fruit of the Burmese Tree of Heaven, along with coconut, mango, breadfruit, durian, mushrooms, turmeric, paprika, ginger'—and a hundred other spices and oils you've never heard of, which I'm skipping over—'and including a tincture of the skin secretions of the Flamboyant Heart frog, the pureed venom sac of the Bengal viper, and the ground claws of the Sumatran skink. It is so exquisite that when it is eaten by one with a palate refined to perfection by years of study, it sometimes happens that the third bite will be fatal. However, the one tasting it will pass away with an indescribable smile of peace on his lips. Serve over rice.'" Sandy closed the book. "What do you think?"

"Darling, but…" said Phinny, standing up quickly from her desk.

Sandy, stepping to her in a rush, folded her in his ample arms like a friendly bear—he had added quite a few pounds over the years. "Darling," he said, "I know what you're think-ing. What if...What if...But what if I don't? What if I don't try it? I'll be a broken man, a beaten food explorer. I'll have to hang up my combination spoon, fork, and knife. I'll end my days on a large sofa, with a heated frozen dinner on my spin-dly knees, watching daytime game shows with a faraway look in my eyes, gibbering, gibbering, What if...What if..."

Sandy hugged Phinny tighter, who squeaked a bit. "I've got to try it!"

He tried it.

And on the third bite, Sandy, with an indescribable smile of peace on his lips, was welcomed by the angels.

Brother Walter was very helpful. All the monks, in fact, as-sured and reassured and re-reassured Phinny that this was the greatest possible outcome for Sandy and each of the monks themselves aspired to this end. Still, Phinny was left heartbro-ken without Sandy. He had passed down an avenue she was not yet prepared to take.

"Would you like to take him home with you?" Brother Walter asked. When Phinny nodded quietly, he said, "Wait here." Then the monks sang and chanted for seven days, at the end of which time they presented Phinny with a kind of casserole dish of Sandy's ashes.

It took another couple of months for Phinny and Sandy to get home. When they did, most of the residents of 777 were gathered in the lobby and Otis's door stood open.

When Phinny, her family around her, Sandy in her arms, stepped into Elevator Number Two, sometimes called Otis, and turned to face the door, the bell that usually rang quietly only once to announce the door's closing rang slowly, loudly, sadly three times, once for Sandy, once for Phinny, and once for Otis himself, before the door rolled softly shut.

The usual two-minute ride to the penthouse took four and the ceiling light stayed dim.

Sandy's ashes were sprinkled among the shrubbery on the north terrace. Many of the building residents had tea on the south terrace. Later, Phinny stepped into the elevator to escape the well-wishing crowd and rode up and down to have a bit of a cry with Otis.

There was a long, a very long silence in the building manager's office.

"So you see, Mrs. MacDougal," said the building manager at last, rearranging a few more reports on his desk, "old Mrs. Rotterdam-Bottom will never allow Elevator Number Two, sometimes called Otis, to be modernized. Not," the building manager leaned forward, "until after she pushes her own last call button."

Mrs. MacDougal picked at a little pill of wool on the front of her sweater. She pressed her lips together and sniffed. However, she had nothing to say.

ANNA AND PEE WEE

WHEN ANNA Brownback was quite a young mouse, she took to sleeping in the box of tissues that always stood on a small table next to a long leather couch. The tissue box, the table, and the long leather couch were part of the furnishings of the consulting room of Dr. Otto Ackerman, the great psychoanalyst. We at 777 Garden Avenue were all proud to know that Dr. Ackerman had his consulting room on the fourth floor of our building.

Inside the box of tissues it was warm, dark, and soft—perfect for a mouse—and the low voices that mumbled one after another in a nearly continuous ribbon of sound somewhere over Anna's head contributed to the delicious atmosphere of the place. The tissue box always stood in the same spot each morning and was never allowed to be empty of tissues. Dr. Ackerman's housekeeper saw to that: a full box, in the same spot, to start each day.

True, a long-fingered hand would occasionally yank the top tissue away, sending Anna rolling, but these little interruptions were worth the luxuriousness of the thing and even added to some of the romance. If Anna had listened to what the voices said immediately after she took a tumble she might have heard something like this:

"Oh, doctor, *warmed* facial tissues! That's so nice. You *are* thoughtful."

In reply, Dr. Ackerman merely nodded, smug in the knowledge that, of course he *was* thoughtful, but somewhere in the back of his mind he was not entirely sure precisely what his patient was referring to.

And Dr. Ackerman did like to be precise.

Had he but looked, he would have found that it was precisely due to a mouse who had just been sleeping on the tissue in question, warming it with her little warm-blooded rodent's heart, and his scientific mind would have rested easier.

But Dr. Ackerman never did look.

He never looked into the tissue box.

It was Anna who looked out of the tissue box.

It was, after all, inevitable that Anna would become curious about the owners of the voices she heard murmuring all day, and so one morning she cautiously peeked out.

What she saw surprised her.

A woman lay on her back on the long black couch, her head resting on a pillow near the tissue box. She spoke in a soft voice, like a large pot on a very low simmer, bubble, bubble, pop. And then she reached for a tissue and blew her nose loudly into it. Anna had quickly stepped out of the way into the darkness of the tissue-box corner when this happened.

And so it went throughout the day. Each hour someone new arrived, men, women, even children. All stretched out on the couch. Some spoke loudly, others whispered, and some hardly spoke at all but merely reached for the tissues.

Dr. Ackerman was mostly silent. Instead of speaking he

nodded, or made a note in a small red notebook that he held in his lap.

Formerly, their voices had come to Anna as she lay, tucked into a corner of the tissue box, as a river of sound. But now curious, Anna concentrated on what the voices were actually saying.

They were telling stories.

Sometimes one person told one, or two, or even three stories in his or her hour. Sometimes the stories lasted for hour after hour, each installment picking up where the last session ended.

And Anna became fascinated by them.

And then Anna began to take notes herself.

And that's how Anna became the first mouse psychiatrist with a practice at 777 Garden Avenue.

When Dr. Ackerman's last client closed the apartment door behind him, and Dr. Ackerman stood up from his chair and stretched, and then shuffled into his kitchen to make himself a cup of tea and look through the containers of leftover take-out Thai food in his refrigerator, Anna crept out of the tissue box and crawled down the electrical cord of the table lamp to the floor where she ran along the baseboard till she came to the hole next to the hot-water pipes.

Her own office stood about a yard from the water pipes, in a cozy abscess halfway up the plaster wall. In her office the couch was made from an unwanted telephone directory, one of several she found stacked in the mail room. Anna had opened the directory to the G's and then munched up the insides to make a lovely soft spot, almost like a nest really. She sat on an old wooden spool herself.

Her first clients were her brothers and sisters of course (she had seven): Anton, Anastasia, Alice, Adam, Alexander, Abe, and Agnes.

Through their own stories they told her their troubles,

their worries, their hopes, and their professional goals. They described their dreams and fears. Anna did what Dr. Ackerman always did. She listened, took notes, and made a small comment now and then, saying what her clients perhaps knew already. Still, it was important that she confirmed their mousey hunches.

Anna knew her greatest asset was her ability to sit quietly (not a natural ability for a mouse) and focus her attention on someone else's story, only speaking when something particularly important came to her or was staring her in the face.

Before long, rodents from as far away as the sixth floor, and even the nineteenth, and then the whole building, made appointments to visit Anna once or twice a week. One rat even came from the basement.

So you see the human residents could have quite a strong influence on the animal population of 777 Garden Avenue.

Something similar happened with Pee Wee Brownback, a distant cousin of Anna's.

Like Anna, and like all mice really, Pee Wee was a great sleeper and loved to find the perfect spot for this activity. In Anna's case, it was Dr. Ackerman's tissue box. In Pee Wee's case, it was inside the double bass of the jazz musician Shadow Sorenson, who lived next door to Otto Ackerman. A double bass, more simply called a bass, is an enormous instrument made mostly of finely crafted and oiled wood. It is hollow, but with two oddly shaped holes in its front to allow the vibrations of sound to come out and resonate more strongly. They are shaped like the letter f, lowercase and fancy, and one of them is backward, and they are called "f-holes." Now, if you are a particularly dexterous mouse and not too fat either, you can clamber up and then slide through one of these f-holes into the insides of the instrument.

As your mouse eyes blink, quickly adjusting to the changed

light inside, you'll see light filtering dustily through the f-holes into a grand space, like the nave of a Gothic cathedral, or the hull of an upturned boat.

Pee Wee loved this place from the instant he saw it.

And just as he was settling down for his first nap of the day, the whole thing moved, lifting up and then standing upright and swaying slightly.

Pee Wee had curled up in the soft roundness at what was now the bottom of the double bass. He popped his head up to see what might happen next.

A tuneful thumping came through the wood, a vibration that made everything, including Pee Wee, shiver. The vibrations changed, rising and falling. Pee Wee trembled. Pee Wee's big ears got bigger. The vibrations went up and down his tail and then all the way to the tip of his nose. At first, Pee Wee didn't know what he was hearing. But as the minutes went by, and his tail started swinging, and his big ears began to lean forward, trying to guess which way the next sound would go, Pee Wee knew what it was. It was music. His sleeping spot, the double bass, was making music. And because he was inside the bass, Pee Wee felt like he was inside the music itself.

Pee Wee wouldn't sleep any more that day.

Instead, he listened to the sounds, the music. As Shadow Sorenson plucked his bass, the gentle thumpings ran up or down. Pee Wee felt it all through the pads in his feet and his sensitive ears. When the thumpings ended, Pee Wee was momentarily dismayed. But then a new sound, a humming, began, much louder than the thumpings. It was smooth and the sound didn't stop. Again, sometimes the sounds went up and sometimes down, louder, then softer. It was like a river or the sea. It was beautiful.

Pee Wee felt like he was in heaven.

Then he heard a distant sound, a clatter, more thumps, less

tuneful though, and then voices, human voices, low and high, quite a few. Pee Wee hung on with his toenails as the whole double bass was put down on its side. He crawled back up to one of the f-holes and peeked out.

Several people had arrived in Shadow's apartment, all carrying oddly shaped boxes, which they set down around them, shaking hands and slapping one another's backs.

Soon Shadow's friends (Pee Wee could tell they were friends) were opening the boxes and removing all kinds of oddly shaped things. Some bright and shiny full of looping metal coils, or odd holes, a couple looking like small versions of the wonderful thing Pee Wee was in, Shadow's bass. Pee Wee began to get curious about how the sleeping might be in one of them, when his own sleeping spot lifted up, sending him scrambling again for a place to hang on to.

Pee Wee could only hope that the thumpings would begin anew, and they did, but to Pee Wee's astonishment, and joy, more thumpings, mewings, hummings, and liquidy shoutings began all around him until he was surrounded by a sea of sound, moving in different directions but together, swinging like a contented cat.

That was the night Pee Wee became a jazz musician. When at last, hours later, the music had stopped, and the others had gone, and even Shadow Sorenson had brushed his teeth and gone to bed, Pee Wee crept out of the left f-hole, ran along the carpet, over the threshold to the kitchen and in behind the stove, through a hole, then down along several long tunnels, and at last to the bunch of chambers in the wall where he lived.

All the next day, he couldn't sleep. Instead, he brooded on the best way to make his own mouse-size double bass. He spent a couple of nights gathering the materials. His bass would be constructed out of two oatmeal boxes (which he craftily gnawed), a tongue depressor, a small shell, and some

broken ukulele strings—a real find. Lurking in the hall garbage closet had really paid off for Pee Wee.

Pee Wee settled in to study jazz. Day and night, for weeks,
Pee Wee Brownback sat inside Shadow Sorenson's double
bass, listening to every note and every silence, learning jazz
from the inside. Sometimes Pee Wee even left 777 Garden
Avenue, traveling with Shadow in his double bass to jazz clubs
and restaurants, even some concert halls, getting a crazy jazz
education.

During the day, the inspiration of the night before sent Pee
Wee practicing on his oatmeal-box bass, refining the instrument and his facility on it.

After the first weeks of study and practice passed, Pee Wee
was showing other mice, notably his brother, Spitball, how to
build and play their own instruments, with the result that, in
the late fall of that year, Pee Wee had assembled a classic five-
piece ensemble. They began gigging every night.

And that's when Pee Wee got the first complaints about the
noise. They came from his upstairs neighbor and distant
cousin, Anna Brownback. Anna and Pee Wee lived within the
wall that separated Otto Ackerman's and Shadow Sorenson's
apartments, in chambers one above the other.

Anna stood in Pee Wee's doorway.

"Excuse me," said Anna, "but the noise is disturbing my
patients."

"It's not noise," said Pee Wee, "it's music."

"Whatever you call it, we can hear it upstairs, and frankly,
it's unsettling to my patients."

"Won't you come in?" said Pee Wee.

Anna hesitated at the door. "I have another session in forty-
five minutes."

"Plenty of time for a cup of Earl Grey."

While Pee Wee moved about in the kitchen, Anna sat down in the living hole and looked around her. After a once-over of the perimeter, she let her eyes rest on the centerpiece of the room, Pee Wee's double bass.

"What's this?" she said.

Pee Wee, poking his head in from the kitchen, said, "That's my double bass. I'm a jazz bassist."

"I see," said Anna. "Tell me how you feel about this bass."

"I love it," said Pee Wee, returning with the tea and cookie bits. "It's my life. It's everything to me, baby. You dig?"

"Of course I dig. I am a mouse. I also rustle and gnaw. But why do you call me 'baby,' when you can see that I am a fully grown mouse? Why this infantilization?"

"Milk? Sugar, sugar?" said Pee Wee.

"Very interesting. Thank you for the tea, by the way. Apparently this music, this jazz, so-called, has not completely uncivilized you," said Anna, nodding with an approving eye at the tea and cookie bits.

"Au contraire, grizzly bear. Jazz is civilization." Putting down his teacup, Pee Wee jumped up to his bass. "Listen." Pee Wee leaned into the instrument, closed his eyes, breathed in deeply through his long sensitive nose, and, with an exhalation, played, "Bom bom bom beem boom bah bam bee ba-boom bah. Bom bom bom beem boom-bah bah bah BAH ba. Bom bom bom beem boom bam bam (bam bam bam bam) bam bam beem beem bam bam bam."

As he played, his whiskers trembled and his tail twitched languidly on the backbeat.

"Those were the opening measures of Thelonious Monk's "Round Midnight.' That's civilization, man."

Anna sipped her tea and set it down, wiping her mouth discreetly with the back of her paw.

"Now you address me as 'man.' I am a mouse, as you can see."

"Oh, sorry, chickadee—ooh!"

"Whether a bird is closer to a mouse than a human is debatable. Listen, I thank you for the cup of tea and this most interesting discussion. I think I could write several articles about it. However, the purpose of my visit remains the same. Do I have your assurance that this music, or jazz, or civilization, whatever nomenclature you prefer, will come to an end?"

"Come to an end?"

"Finish. Cease. Yes."

"Cease!"

"And stop."

"Stop! Listen, you mad mouse witch doctor. I will not finish, I don't care to cease, and I've never heard the word *stop* before in my life. You call yourself a doctor! How can you help patients if you have no feeling for music? Music is medicine for your heart. It's what keeps it healthy. You must have no heart!"

"What!"

"That's right. No heart!"

"Why, you uncivilized, spoiled, infantile—"

"That's uncool, man."

"—ignorant, louche, gauche, crass—"

"Very uncool."

Still muttering unflattering adjectives, Anna scuttled out of the room, slamming the door behind her.

And so the painful matter rested.

Pee Wee refused to stop playing. If anything, he played longer, and played louder.

Anna found three more books of yellow pages and, tearing

them up, and chewing them a bit till she had a hardy mass of mortar, plugged every little crack or seam that might let in sound from Pee Wee's apartment.

It wasn't a particularly friendly arrangement on either side, but this is how they kept it for the next three weeks, which is fairly long in mouse time.

And so the situation might have stayed except for two unexpected developments.

For the first time in his career, Pee Wee Brownback got stage fright. Up till now, when faced with a roomful of curious rodents, Pee Wee bounded into it, eager to share his music with any critter. But now, as his fame in the building had grown, he began to be afraid of disappointing his fans, of letting down his bandmates. In short, he feared failure. Finally, one night, in the middle of his solo in "One O'Clock Jump," Pee Wee had suddenly become frozen. He couldn't find the next note. His paws curled uselessly over the fingerboard. He did not know what to do. After a couple of anxious measures, Spitball took over with an impromptu drum solo. Pee Wee stood as if fixed, pinned to a board, only his tail switched herky-jerkily back and forth.

From that point on, Pee Wee dreaded that this might happen again. Now, before every concert, his paws sweated. His whiskers gyrated madly. His mouse heart, already beating the normal mouse five hundred beats per minute, now shot up to a dangerous seven hundred and fifty.

Finally, the piano player, Fats Whiterback, took Pee Wee aside and said, "Hey, mouse. This is uncool. You've got to see someone about this. I think I know just the cat, pardon the expression. It's a bird, actually. Dr. Anna Brownback. She's the

McShizz for all your mental problems. My brother-in-law went to see her. He's not nearly so nuts now." Slapping Pee Wee on the back, Fats Whiterback said, "Seriously, before the concert tomorrow night, see Dr. Brownback."

Anna Brownback opened her study door to an unanticipated knock. There, on her doorstep, stood Pee Wee.

"You!" said Anna.

"Yup," said Pee Wee, holding his tail between his paws and kneading it.

"How can I help you," said Anna, not inviting him in.

"I'm here for a session. I need your professional help," said Pee Wee.

"Not a friendly neighborly call, then."

"Not exactly."

"Lie down on the yellow pages." Anna picked up her notebook and pencil. "What is troubling you?"

Pee Wee burrowed a bit in the litter of the chewed pages, then poked his head up, a few bits of paper clinging to his ears. "I get so nervous now before a performance, I can't play my bass."

"How too disappointing."

Pee Wee looked into Anna's large eyes.

"I'm serious! This is serious. Doctor, are you going to help me or not?"

Anna looked at Pee Wee for a long minute. She smoothed her whiskers back along her left side and then down her right. She put down her notebook and looked at Pee Wee again.

"Please, lie down. Soothe yourself. Of course, I will help you. That is my job. That is my profession." She took a breath and rearranged herself on her spool. Then she looked sternly at Pee Wee and said, "You are simply suffering from too much caring. You have a big heart. You care too much about letting your audience down. It is perfectly natural in someone of your description. I noticed it right away when I saw you. Heart's too big. Heart won't listen to reason."

Pee Wee lay for a moment slack-jawed and then said, "But what can I do? I have to play the bass!"

Anna picked up her notebook and wrote a few lines in it. She said, "Here's what I recommend. Every evening, before a performance, read two pages of the *Encyclopedia Britannica*. Do you have it?"

"Yeah, I have volume eleven. I use it to make bedding."

"Good. But don't sleep on it anymore. No, you must stop that. Now you must read it. Two pages. This will increase your brain and shrink your heart at the same time. So next time you feel an attack of nerves coming on, your brain can simply take over and tell yourself that you have nothing to worry about."

Pee Wee thanked Anna Brownback. But he left her study with his shoulders still slumped, doubtful about her suggested remedy. Nevertheless, arriving in his hole, Pee Wee read his two pages of the encyclopedia. And to Pee Wee's delight, the next night at the concert he didn't get nervous. His brain talked and his heart listened. He felt great. His playing was perhaps a little cooler than in the old days, but that was fine. Fats Whiterback, too, was impressed with Pee Wee's night, especially his virtuosic two-claw plucking passages.

The second unexpected event to unsettle Pee Wee and Anna's status quo came two nights later, on the one night a week Pee Wee had off. That night, he was lounging, thinking about the past few days, when he was surprised by a knock at his door, and then even more surprised when he saw who was standing on his doorstep.

"Dr. Brownback!"

"May I come in?" said Anna.

"Sure, I'll make tea," said Pee Wee.

"No, thank you. And, please, call me Anna." Anna walked quietly to the living room and sat down.

"I've been meaning to thank you for your help," said Pee Wee. "It worked right away."

"I am glad," said Anna. She scratched behind her ear with a large hind foot. "The thing is," she said quietly, "I've been having trouble relating to my clients. This afternoon I wanted to stop a particular mouse from complaining so much. That wouldn't be so bad, but I wanted to stop her complaining with a carving knife!"

"Like the farmer's wife," said Pee Wee.

"Pardon? Anyway, all these rodents, one after another, telling me their troubles, and waiting for me to help them! And for the first time in my career, I don't much care if I help them or not. So you see?"

"I see," said Pee Wee. "What I don't see, however, is why you've come to me."

"Well," said Anna, assuming the brusque tone of her first visit. "Yes. Certainly, it is unusual. Naturally, I have spoken with my colleagues. That's the first thing I did. But frankly, I did not receive from them a great deal of understanding. Nor much useful help. Oh, we're a macho crowd, we mouse psychiatrists. In fact, some mouse psychiatrists I know are downright heartless..." Anna's voice trailed away and she gnawed in a distraught way at a toenail.

Pee Wee's dark brown eyes shone a little more brightly.

"And then I remembered," said Anna in a voice just above a whispered squeak, "what you said about my own heart."

Pee Wee, sitting down next to Anna on the sofa, took one of her paws in his. He looked into Anna's light brown eyes and said, "You're worried, with all of your calmness and reasonableness and so forth, that your heart has gotten too small."

"That's it!" said Anna. "Oh, please, help me, help me! Make my heart bigger!"

"I know just the thing," said Pee Wee.

Later that evening, Anna, following Pee Wee, crawled into the outside pocket of Shadow Sorenson's bass bag and burrowed in among the old candy wrappers and rosin boxes.

"What's that smell?" said Anna.

"I think it's a little bit of chocolate mashed up in the wrappers," said Pee Wee. "We might have a lick."

"No, that other smell."

"Oh, that's the rosin. It's what bass players use to make their bows sticky. It's like a kind of rock."

Pee Wee knew that on the one night Shadow didn't play in a jazz band, he played as a substitute in the bass section of the New York Philharmonic. Pee Wee had made the trip to the concert hall with him a couple of times before.

"It's not too far," Pee Wee explained. "And remember, we're perfectly safe in the bass bag. It's when we get to the concert hall that things get a little touch and go. Still, it will be worth it for the sake of your heart."

As a matter of fact, the trip was somewhat long. It involved a subway, a bus, and lots of rolling along the sidewalk. But when they arrived at Lincoln Center, where the New York

Philharmonic performs, and made their first nose-pokings out of the bass pocket, Anna was agog. The crowds of elegant people. The sound they made. The lights all around them. And the smells.

"Pretty great, right?" said Pee Wee.

"Right."

"Wait till you see the hall. Wait until you see our seats!"

After Shadow Sorenson extracted his bass, Anna followed Pee Wee carefully out of the bag. They ran along the walls of the dressing room and along the back corridors of the theater behind the stage. Pee Wee seemed unconcerned about being spotted by anyone.

"There's loads of local mice here," he shouted over his shoulder. "No one will worry about a couple of extras."

When they passed an elderly mouse sauntering by in the other direction, Pee Wee wished him a cordial "Good evening," but the elderly mouse hardly noticed.

On the threshold of the stage entrance they stopped. Anna blinked and blinked at the bright white-and-gold light making everything in the enormous room sparkle.

"Okay, now," said Pee Wee. "Here's the tricky bit. Better take ahold of my tail."

Anna did. And then, by quick dashes, from one chair leg to another, along and under music stands, past a couple of cellos lying on their sides, they stopped just under the conductor's podium.

"These are great seats!" said Anna, panting a bit.

"We're not there yet. Just wait, I'm taking you to the luxury box."

They waited in the deep shadow of the podium as musicians stepped onto the stage, finding their chairs, chatting with someone in the second violins, or sharing a joke in the trombone section. There was much honking and scraping of instruments—"noodling" is the technical term.

"Is this the music?" said Anna.

"No, no, they're just warming up. Wait, here comes our seat."

A queenly-looking woman, her golden hair piled in coils on the crown of her lofty head, was moving, like a yacht cruising into its home port, down the center aisle. At the very first row she turned to her left and gracefully sidled over. She eased into her plush seat. Loosening her rich sable coat—Pee Wee had never seen her without it—she slipped it off her shoulders, but let it still cradle her in its warmth.

"Now comes the really tricky bit. Follow me closely. Take my tail. You'll need all your claws for this so hold it in your mouth."

Anna, clinging with her incisors a little too tightly to Pee Wee's tail—Pee Wee was too polite really to complain—tried to keep her little mouse heart from beating right out of her chest. Pee Wee ran along the edge of the podium, his whole svelte body very close to the floor. Then he scrambled over and down the front wall of the stage, clinging to a vertical crack where the sections of wooden paneling met.

This was all done in the couple of seconds that the lady's head was turned strongly to the left, where she discussed something with her neighbor.

Now under her seat, Pee Wee and Anna paused for breath. When Anna had nodded to indicate she was ready, Pee Wee flung himself up into the folds of the lady's fur coat. As Anna followed and began climbing, she could hear the sound of the lady's high-pitched and excited nasal voice grow louder.

"And then her cell phone rang in the middle of it and I could have just died. It was too..." The lady's voice cascaded down.

Anna's heart beat harder and louder as they carefully clambered up the coat.

"So I said to her..." came shrill and loud in Anna's fine ears.

At last Pee Wee whispered, "In here," and they both tumbled into the right-hand pocket of the coat, in among silk gloves and a fine scented handkerchief.

As Pee Wee arranged the gloves and handkerchief to his liking, he said, "Pretty deluxe, no?"

"Yes, it is," said Anna, trying to recover her breath. "Wait a second."

Anna began sniffing around the pocket, especially the scented handkerchief. Then she carefully peeked out of the pocket at the lady, returning almost immediately to Pee Wee's side.

"I know this lady," she said. "She's Dr. Ackerman's two o'clock on Thursdays."

"Well, she's also the Philharmonic's eight o'clock on Wednesdays."

"What if the lady finds us in here? Won't she make a fuss?"

"If she sticks her hand in, first hide in the corner, but if she does happen to touch you, just act like a fur coat, and she'll never notice."

"Yes, that can work," said Anna, remembering Dr. Ackerman's tissue box.

Pee Wee smiled. "But that's never happened yet. She falls asleep in the first two minutes."

Outside the pocket, the roarishness of the human voices was beginning to diminish. Anna and Pee Wee cautiously poked their noses out of the pocket. The lights of the hall had dimmed. By contrast, the lights directed onto the stage seemed indescribably dazzling, sending flashes of fiery light from each reflected French horn, piccolo, and cuff link. The wood of the stringed instruments glowed in warm browns and reds and near blacks.

Then a fine-looking man in a tuxedo strode quickly across the stage, stopping briefly to shake the concertmaster's hand, and stepped onto the podium: the conductor.

Waiting for what would come next, Anna breathed in the rich symphony of smells that washed through her, exploding almost like fireworks in her nose. The rosin, the oiled woods and brasses, the wood of the stage, the thick velvet of the seats, the scent of the fur coat, and the lady's elegant perfume, and even the rising smell of the musicians, as they began to sweat in anticipation of the evening's work.

The conductor raised his baton and the smell of sweat rose with it.

Suddenly down came the baton, and the curling wave of sound that it unleashed knocked Anna tail over head back down into the luxurious pocket.

"It's too much! It's too much!" said Anna. "I think my heart will break!"

Pee Wee reached a paw down to Anna and pulled her back up. "Don't worry, it's just Brahms. You always feel that way with Brahms."

Pee Wee and Anna spent the rest of the evening hand in hand—that is, paw in paw—in the fur coat's pocket. Anna's heart grew larger in the first movement, broke in the second, healed during the third, and then split in half all over again in the fourth movement of Brahms's Fourth Symphony, but then what mouse heart wouldn't? Even a rational heart like Anna's can't withstand Brahms when it is that close.

By the time they reached 777 Garden Avenue late that night, both hearts were mended, their neighborly feud was over, and before the first crocuses of spring had poked up their heads in the tree pits, Anna and Pee Wee had moved up to the eleventh floor into the walls of Miss Nancy's apartment where there was space enough for a music studio, rooms for patients, and a nice cozy den for when their first litter would arrive at the beginning of the summer.

THE BOILER

"WRENCH."

"Wrench."

"Needle-nose pliers."

"Needle-nose pliers."

"Sponge."

"Sponge."

Our building attendant, or super, Oskar, withdrew the upper portion of his blue-overalled body from a spaghetti bowl of copper tubing, oily bulbous receptacles, and silver faucet handles, and sat on his heels. He reached to his back pocket, pulling out a greasy handkerchief, and wiped his brow.

"How is she?" said Victoria.

"Oh, old Liesl has seen worse trouble in her time. Looks to me like all she needs is a new ancillary intake valve."

"That sounds serious," said Victoria, now wiping her brow with her own handkerchief.

"No, not really. It's pretty routine," said the super. "So long as we get a valve that fits, Old Liesl will be almost good as new."

"Almost?" said Victoria, with a worried look on her small heart-shaped face.

"Well, I'm a little worried about a possible blockage of her pipes. Up on the fifteenth floor. If that's the case there could be a big blow, or what's maybe worse, the blockage could dislodge itself and travel all the way down here to Liesl herself and then she could get constipated and even crack."

Victoria stepped back two paces and looked up at the enormous machine looming over her. A big tank, like a giant headache pain-relief capsule, stood on four legs, rumbling and hissing. The whole thing was painted deep carmine red. At one end several large pipes rose into the ceiling. At the other the spaghetti bowl of smaller pipes emerged, connecting the tank with a many-cornered metal box. This is our boiler. It gives us steam heat in the winter and hot water for our sinks and tubs all year long.

"Let's go take a look at the fifteenth floor."

Ever since she could remember, Victoria had been interested in plumbing. Why this was so, she wasn't sure. Possibly, it was when she lost her favorite plastic pink ring, the one with the butterfly stone, down the bathroom sink, and Oskar, by the simple procedure of unscrewing the cleanout plug on the bottom of the sub-sink trap, had found it and returned the ring to her that her fascination had begun.

You can't go from the utter depths of black despair, convinced in your heart of hearts that you will never see your plastic pink ring, the one with the butterfly stone, ever again, and then arrive at the Olympic heights of bliss when Oskar calmly hands you the very same plastic pink ring with the butterfly stone, saying, "There you are, Miss Victoria, good as new," without it having a pretty profound effect on your overall worldview, when you're three.

This had led Victoria to see Oskar as some sort of superman

and she immediately took a strong interest in his doings. Not long after this, she was well rewarded when a mysterious leak was discovered emanating from some spot between her floor, floor ten, and the floor above.

Oskar had arrived, walked purposefully to the hall closet of their apartment, and, to Victoria's immense surprise, removed a board in the back, thereby revealing an array of beautiful shining, convoluted and involuted pipes and valve hand wheels. Quite literally an unseen world had opened before her. She had immediately asked what was what, what went where, and so on. Happily, Oskar is not a super who doesn't like to answer questions. So he spoke of risers and descenders, showed Victoria which pipes were cold and which were hot, and then gave her his best estimate as to where exactly the leak was.

Later that day Victoria watched the hole get knocked into the wall in the inside stairs. Oskar then showed her with his flashlight how the hole in the wall in the stairs could actually lead up to the inside of her own closet.

"It's Main Street for mice. Not that this building has any mice, of course," said Oskar, quickly.

"Thank goodness for that," said Victoria. "I'm afraid of mice."

Since that time Victoria had been fascinated by the insides of the building that we don't see: the pipes, the beams, the cables. She started to accompany Oskar on his rounds whenever she could.

But back to our story of Liesl, our boiler. The winter of Victoria's tenth year was an extremely cold one. Arctic winds picked up from their accustomed playgrounds in northern Canada and hustled south, around and over the Adirondack Mountains, and then down the Hudson River valley, which funneled them like some geographic tollbooth plaza until the winds arrived furious and biting in the streets of Manhattan, Brooklyn, Queens, the Bronx, and Staten Island.

But especially Manhattan because everything is at its utmost in Manhattan.

Then 777 Garden Avenue shivered. And the residents inside shivered too. Something was wrong with Liesl. All the outside rooms of the building were cold.

"Liesl is depressed," said Oskar, as he and Victoria walked the hallway on the eighth floor. They had found no blockages on the fifteenth floor. "Her extremities are cold. She's got bad circulation. She's not digesting properly."

They stopped at 8D, Mr. Sherman's apartment, and rang the bell.

Mr. Sherman opened the door. He stood in a bathrobe, woolen gray slippers, and a ski hat with earflaps.

"Er," said Oskar, "sorry to disturb, but we're checking all the radiators."

"Hi, Mr. Sherman," said Victoria.

"It's like the North Pole in here," said Mr. Sherman. "I should drill a hole in my living-room floor and go ice fishing. I have to put my head in the toaster oven just to think."

Oskar and Victoria slid past Mr. Sherman, who followed them into the living room.

"Can I feel my fingertips? Forget about it! I can't feel my elbows. There's a sign in the back of my mouth that says 'Danger: Bridge Frozen!' The cockroaches have formed a hockey league in the kitchen sink."

Oskar kneeled down and placed his hand on the radiator and then turned the valve wheel back and forth a bit, holding his ear close to it. He held up a hand to stop Mr. Sherman from talking.

Victoria stooped over Oskar and Mr. Sherman stooped over Victoria.

Then they all three straightened and retraced their steps to the front door.

Mr. Sherman said, "Don't you want to take the temperature of my bed? It's like the cold of deep space. It's like the far side of the moon. You seen that documentary about the emperor penguins in Antarctica? That's my bedroom on a good day! Look, it's so cold my hair won't grow. I'm going bald. I have to wear this hat."

"You've always been bald, Mr. Sherman," said Victoria.

"Yeah, maybe, but not this bald," and Mr. Sherman pulled off his ski hat like a conjuror revealing the rabbit and inclined his bald pate toward Victoria.

As a matter of fact, his head did look particularly bald.

"Thanks, Mr. Sherman," said Oskar. "We're working on it. Good afternoon, Mr. Sherman."

"Next time you visit," said Mr. Sherman, "bring a cocktail shaker. You can use bits and pieces of my frozen body to chill the gin." Then he shook Victoria's hand, saying, "Nice to see you, Victoria. Say hello to your mother." And he shut the door.

Walking to the elevator, Victoria said, "His hands really are cold."

"We've got to get through to Liesl somehow. She's losing the will to live. And she's too young to die. She's only twenty-five years old."

Victoria's eyes began to lose focus, then rolled gently upward, and at last snapped open like two mousetraps and refocused when some inner alarm pulled her back into consciousness.

She sat, leaning forward over a sheet of paper, the third handout her fourth-grade teacher, Ms. Emily Bland, had dealt the class that day.

Victoria read:

Read the following text fragment and then write a sentence about how the text fragment makes you feel, using the phrase, "The description of the mountains makes me feel _____ and _____."

I feel terrible, thought Victoria. I can't see straight, my fingers and toes are freezing, something's wrong in my stomach. Am I losing the will to live?

Victoria pushed herself back from her desk and folded her arms, a deep and thoughtful frown spreading across her face. Normally an assignment like "The description of the mountains makes me feel _____ and _____," while certainly annoying, wouldn't cause her to lose the will to live. It was just a part of the routine of her day. There must be something more bothering her. She thought back.

She had felt fine in the morning. Gym had been okay. Math was fun, even. Social studies had been engaging. So why had one simple black-and-white handout given her such a feeling of doom?

Victoria squeezed her eyes shut. The first bad feelings had come to her just after lunch. What had happened at lunch? She had sat with the usual pals, eating the usual lunch: peanut butter and salami with iceberg lettuce on rye, an apple, a cookie, and a pint of milk.

All correct. Or was it? There was something that was wrong. Victoria could nearly taste it. She took a deep breath, relaxed her brow, and then she remembered. The milk was wrong. It was skim! She usually drank whole milk. Today her usual red container was the palest blue. Of course! It had tasted awful. But was this the solution?

One minute before the bell for dismissal rang, Victoria carefully wrote in, "The description of the mountains makes me feel weak and disoriented, unable to focus and get on with my life," and passed it over to Ms. Bland, as she came around the desks to collect the papers.

Five minutes later, out on the narrow and crowded sidewalk of Lexington Avenue, Victoria checked her change purse for funds.

"A dollar thirty-five. Plenty," she said, cupping her hand over the purse and pushing into the door of the U Like Deli. At the back of the store she grabbed an ice-cold pint of milk in the sweating red carton, paid, and then drank it down in one go on the sidewalk, in spite of the icy winds blowing around her, tickling the fake fur of her quilted hoodie.

"Shazam! Low-fat begone, I feel good."

Fully recovered by dinnertime, she ate, watched a little TV, did her homework, and crawled into bed early. It was just too darn cold in the apartment to stay up any longer.

The rest of the week continued as before. The arctic winds blew and the outside rooms were, if anything, getting colder. Mr. Sherman had taken to pacing the lobby in his bathrobe, slippers, hat, and coat.

"Eskimos," he said, "have twenty-nine different names for cold. Number twenty-three is umlukniknob, which, translated into English, means 'my living room.' "

Oskar handed Victoria a mug of hot cocoa and they sat down across from each other at his metal-topped desk in his office in the basement, just down the hall from where Liesl stood on her spindly but sturdy legs, softly hissing and murmuring.

"The board meets tomorrow night. If I can't figure out what's bothering Liesl by then, she's had it. The residents won't put up with this anymore and I don't blame them. She's been a good old boiler, but I guess this is her time."

"This is not her time, Oskar, and you know it," said Victoria, putting her hot cocoa down softly.

"I know! You're right. All right. Now let's just think this through slowly one more time. What does Liesl's day look like? The answer must be there. Well, she never goes out. It's a very quiet life really. She just stands in the room and makes steam. From October to April she makes steam, and then in the summer she gets a bit of a rest. She doesn't see anybody. Except me."

"But are you sure?" said Victoria. "What if someone has been sneaking into Liesl's room and tampering with her? Who besides you has a key to her room?"

"Well, Mr. Zeebruggen, the board president, and the building manager do, but why would they tamper with Liesl? What's their motive?"

"I'm getting to that. First, we establish opportunity. Then we look into motive. Maybe there's something in it for Mr. Zeebruggen, or the building manager, if we get a new boiler. What if one of them is in tight with a boilermaker and will get some kind of kickback if we buy a new one? How much would a new boiler cost?"

"A lot."

"That's it then. We've established motive. And we've got opportunity. Once we connect one of them to the new boiler company..." Her voice trailed off. Then she clapped her hands. "This won't be the first time a little graft, bribery, and corruption have reared their ugly heads."

"Kickbacks? Graft, bribery, and corruption? Where do you learn this stuff?"

"Social studies. Mr. Engbloom believes in telling it like it is." Victoria chewed on the end of a pencil. "Now, we're going to have to break into the building manager's office, and Mr. Zeebruggen's apartment, possibly even hack into their computers, but I'll handle that end. Okay, what time does the building manager call it a night?"

"Six thirty, but hold on now, Miss Victoria. We are not breaking into anyone's office or apartment. That's ridiculous. It's against the law, the building procedures, and my moral principles. Doesn't Mr. Engbloom teach you any moral principles?"

"Mr. Engbloom says we need to return the power to the people."

"Well, Mr. Engbloom does not live at 777 Garden Avenue. Let's leave Mr. Engbloom at school for a minute, because there's another reason your theory is all wrong. I check Liesl every morning myself and all her controls are set properly. There has been no tampering with Liesl. No, let us return once more to Liesl's day. She stands and steams."

Victoria sipped her cocoa. "Well," she said, "if her outsides are right, since you've checked everything, then there must be something wrong with her insides. What goes into Liesl?"

"Water and fuel," said Oskar. "And electricity to regulate her."

"And you say the controls for regulating are correct. The lights down here are all on, so the electricity seems okay. What about the water?"

"Water comes from the water tower, and it's fine. Otherwise we'd all be sick. Liesl drinks the same water we drink."

Victoria put her mug down. "This hot cocoa tastes funny."

"It's low-fat."

"Low-fat. Low-fat? Did you say low-fat? That's it!" Victoria jumped up.

"What's it?"

"Someone's monkeying with her fuel. Listen, I went through this whole same thing at school, but I don't have time to go into it now. When does Liesl get her next drink?"

"Well, she's always drinking. But if you mean when is the next fuel-oil delivery scheduled for, that's tomorrow. It comes in a big truck."

"Perfect. Tomorrow is a teacher-development day. Mr. Engbloom is very excited. Anyway, the important thing is I'll be home and we can stake out Liesl's libation."

"Libation?"

"It means drink. Mr. Engbloom believes in expanding our vocabulary. What's Liesl's libation company, by the way?"

"Lamprey Fuel Oil."

"Maybe I should have Mr. Engbloom check them out. Would it be wrong for me to send him an e-mail, I wonder? I've got to go upstairs. Tomorrow we get to the bottom of this. Don't give up on Liesl!"

The following afternoon, if you had been driving down Seventy-seventh Street on the Upper East Side, you would have had to inch your car past an enormous deep-green tanker truck, double-parked alongside the north side of 777 Garden Avenue. The truck stood yards high and shimmered. It was very clean and the many chrome bits with which it was festooned reflected its yellow lights, its red spiral pinstriping, and its picture of a grinning white lamprey eel.

A heavy hose, the diameter of a medium-size anaconda, ran from the truck's tail end and across half of the sidewalk where it connected to a pipe mouth that ended flush with the sidewalk. This was Liesl's own mouth in a way, where once a month or so she was filled up with fuel, Liesl's libation.

The Lamprey Fuel Oil man lounged against his rumbling green truck, making small talk with Oskar. Victoria, disguised as a ten-year-old too little to be interested in grown-up things, jumped rope in her padded winter parka.

The fuel man strolled over to Victoria.

"Ain't it a little cold to be outside?" he said.

Victoria just stared at him, dumbly.

Oskar said, "I'll head in then. Give me a call when you're finished filling up."

The fuel man nodded to Oskar, turning back to the truck as Oskar glanced at Victoria and raised his left eyebrow before descending the metal ramp to the basement.

Victoria skipped rope.

As soon as Oskar was gone, the fuel man went to the back of the truck and turned a large valve wheel to the right.

Victoria jumped a little closer.

The fuel man unscrewed the metal ring attaching the hose to a spigot on the truck and then shifted it to another spigot next to it. He glanced once over his right shoulder toward the building and then secured the hose to the new spigot. He turned another valve wheel to the left several times and then sauntered to the sidewalk and leaned against the truck again.

Victoria slowly skipped around the corner of the building and then to the front door, where Mr. Bunchley let her in. Immediately, Victoria threw down her jump rope and ran around the elevators to the stairs and then down to the basement.

"Just like I thought," said Victoria, rushing up to Oskar, who was waiting outside the boiler room. "He switched the snake to another hole as soon as you left. I'm sure what he's giving Liesl is low-fat."

"Well, we'll just check that right now."

They entered Liesl's room, climbed five steps of a metal ladder and up to Liesl, who hummed and murmured, smelled like molasses, plums, charcoal, and fire, but still didn't look quite right.

Oskar lifted a pail off of a hook on Liesl's flank.

"Mr. Engbloom sent me a message from his iPhone by the way. Lamprey Fuel Oil has been sued four times since last year."

"We'll have our answer soon," said Oskar, who held the pail beneath a spigot jutting from a large pipe that crossed over to Liesl just below the ceiling.

Oskar pointed over his head. "The Lamprey guy is standing only a few yards that way."

Instinctively, Victoria hid behind Oskar a bit as he slowly opened the spigot with the valve wheel. A stream of what looked like thin Coca-Cola flowed into the pail. Oskar shut the spigot and poured some of the fuel into a glass, which he had taken from a small shelf on the side of the oil tank. He held the glass to the light and then showed it to Victoria. Seen this way, the fuel was very pale indeed. Oskar took a deep sniff at the top of the glass and then offered the glass to Victoria.

Victoria said, "I don't smell anything."

"That's just it," said Oskar. "The smell should just about knock you out." Oskar put the glass on the shelf again and wiped his hands on the rag he took from his back pocket. "It's low-fat, all right. This is diluted fuel. It's weak. They've tampered with her food. They're giving her skim."

Later that evening, Victoria paced outside the building's conference-room door. When it opened at last, Oskar emerged and Victoria walked briskly to him and cocked a questioning eyebrow.

"It's all right. Liesl's safe. We're firing Lamprey Oil and hiring someone else. There's talk of a lawsuit to address the building's pain and suffering."

"Poor Liesl," said Victoria, giving Oskar a big hug around the middle and then skipping down the hall.

One week later, Oskar and Victoria were looking over diagrams of the city's water mains, when a loud banging at his office door made them jump. Oskar opened the door carefully, revealing Mr. Sherman in a Hawaiian shirt, lime green bathing trunks, and purple flip-flops.

Mr. Sherman said, "Have you spent any time in my living room lately? It's like a microwave set to eleven! It's a toaster set on burn! A roaster set to kill! What am I, Kung Pao chicken? My new roommate is a flamingo! Can't you turn the heat down a little?"

HOT WATER

MR. JONES set down his book quietly on the coffee table and placed his hands in his lap.

He said, "Well, I'm off to bed then." Getting up and moving to the hallway, he paused. "Ah," he said, "you'll be able to stop in?"

"As soon as you've brushed your teeth and put on your pj's and so forth, I'll be at your bedside to see to things."

Mr. Jones and Mr. Norton—it was Mr. Norton who had answered—lived in a corner, two-bedroom apartment on the fourth floor at the back of our building. They had been there many years, and theirs was a very happy companionship. Mr. Jones and Mr. Norton suited each other. They were good for each other. They were settled.

This is not to say that they didn't have their difficulties. Mr. Jones was a nervous and fretful person. And, like so many of us as we get older, Mr. Jones began to sleep badly. He was plagued by lack of sleep, a malady that had been familiar to him in his childhood but was all but forgotten in his early active years. A mind that used to be thoroughly exhausted by the events of the day, now found time in the evenings to roam in all the worst dark corners of speculation, remorse, and worry, tormenting its owner with a sleeplessness that might last for days.

Insomnia became Mr. Jones's exquisite torturer. Did Insomnia detect, during the course of a night, a notion in Mr. Jones to get up, fix himself a cup of tea, and watch a little television? Immediately Insomnia advised Mr. Jones to give it just ten more minutes. Insomnia went on to remind Mr. Jones that it was essential, *essential*, that he get his rest, that he sleep *now*, because tomorrow was going to be a big day, requiring all of Mr. Jones's strength. Insomnia assured Mr. Jones that he must try with all of his might to sleep.

And Insomnia chuckled to itself while, instead of finding sleep, Mr. Jones returned to the time of his childhood, when, lying in his bed alone, he listened for the sounds of his family making its way one by one to bed: his older brother turning down his radio and sleeping; his mother putting away her handwork, walking stealthily but not inaudibly past his door to her bed, and sleeping; and finally his father switching off the television and shuffling down the hall to his own bed and sleeping.

And Mr. Jones remembered the moment of greatest terror arriving: Everyone in the house but he, himself, slept. They were gone to another world. Mr. Jones remembered how he was left alone to contemplate the points of dark color that swirled in a soft cyclone around his room, whether his eyes were open or closed. And the smell of the night air, and the touch of the bedclothes, and the sound of distant trucks on the roadways, always driving. That the drivers of those trucks were also awake was of no comfort to Mr. Jones. Quite the contrary, it was merely further proof, if Mr. Jones needed it, that adult life was a brutish and hellish one, forcing men and women from their warm beds to satisfy the needs of others. That this harsh world awaited him was a thing that few children, certainly not he, ever quite forgot.

And so the night was spent.

Mr. Jones rose the next day sick to his stomach, dizzy, and distraught, with his ears burning strangely, and without even memories of late-night television to comfort him.

But now things were different because Mr. Norton had agreed to sit with him.

"Thank you, Norton," said Mr. Jones.

And so they had arranged it each evening.

For instance, if you were in attendance at one of the delightful dinner parties Mr. Jones and Mr. Norton often hosted, even before Mr. Norton had gathered your coats for you and walked you to the elevator, he had always promised Mr. Jones that he would be at his bedside shortly.

"We'll just finish this round, and then I'll be in directly," Mr. Norton might say.

What did Mr. Norton do at Mr. Jones's bedside? Nothing really. He merely sat. He was simply present. He was the face, the body, the hand, the refutation of Mr. Jones's "I am alone." Mr. Norton was the one, and not the zero, that otherwise faced Mr. Jones.

Unfortunately—and here is the blemish in this otherwise idyllic picture—when one man's want is met, when the need is supplied, when the one obliterates the zero, it is all very well for him who receives. But life for the one who provides can get a little boring.

To sit night upon night in a darkened room, admittedly next to someone you love very much, but still, to sit for twenty minutes with only your thoughts for entertainment, thoughts that tended to turn again and again to questions like "Is he asleep yet?" or "Can I get up now?" or "If I stand up at this point, will my rustling wake my friend, sending me back to square one in this game?" or even "Will I have missed the ending to *Star Trek: Deep Space Nine*?" Far from entertaining, these thoughts can be a small torture themselves.

"Jonesy," said Mr. Norton, on that night, sitting in the chair next to Mr. Jones.

"Yes, Norty," said Mr. Jones, arranging his bedclothes.

"Jonesy," said Mr. Norton again. "You know I like to sit with you like this every night, here next to you in this chair."

"Yes, Norty, for which I'm ever thankful."

"And I'm most glad to do it, and am so thankful that you're thankful."

"I'm glad."

"I'm glad you're glad. Still..." Mr. Norton hesitated. He rubbed his mustache. "I've been thinking. I know you like to have me nearby whenever you are falling asleep."

"Yes."

"Here's what I thought." Mr. Norton arranged himself more comfortably on the chair. The bit of light coming in from the hallway picked out his eyebrows, the end of his round nose, and his mustache. He said, "Do you see the wall there, just on the other side of your bed?"

"Why, yes. Yes, of course."

"Well, just on the other side of that wall is our bathroom."

"Really?"

"Yes. And what's more. Right next to the wall on the other side there is our bathtub."

"No kidding."

"What about instead of me sitting here in this chair in the dark, how about I sit in the warm bathtub over there having a soak? I won't be any farther away from you than I am when

I'm sitting in this chair here." (And I'll be able to give my toes a scrub or read the sports section, thought Mr. Norton).

"You mean, instead of you sitting in the chair here, you'll sit in the tub there."

"Exactly."

"But I won't be able to see you."

"Well, no. But you can't really see me now either, can you? It's dark after all. You just know I'm here."

Mr. Jones was silent.

"And you'll be able to see the wall. You'll know I can see the same wall, just from the other side. We'll both be looking at the same single wall. You on this side. Me on that side. Which means I'll still be right next to you. What do you say?"

After a little more discussion, and some almost hidden sighs from Mr. Jones, Mr. Jones and Mr. Norton decided to give it a try the next evening.

That night, Mr. Norton stopped at the doorway of Mr. Jones's room on his way to the tub.

"Well," he said, "I've got my brush and my bar of oatmeal soap, and I'm off to the bath. I think you can hear the water running, can't you?"

"Yes, I can," said Mr. Jones.

"So everything seems all right. All right?"

"Everything is all right, Norty. Right as rain," said Mr. Jones, bravely.

And so it proved to be. Mr. Jones was sound asleep before Mr. Norton had even turned off the hot-water tap. The next morning they had both woken refreshed and Mr. Jones announced that he had rarely slept better. Mr. Norton said that he had thoroughly enjoyed his bath, taking the pumice to his heels and elbows, contemplating the weaknesses in the Yankees' middle roster, and even quoting favorite lines of poetry to no one but his toes:

what Eden is there for the lapsed
but hot water
snug in its caul

The experiment was a success.

A month later it was Mr. Jones who had an idea.

"You know, Norty, I am not what you would call a robust person."

The cracker ascending to Mr. Norton's mouth halted halfway there.

"I am a nervous person," said Mr. Jones.

Mr. Norton bit the cracker, now arrived. "Would you say that?" he mumbled, his mouth full.

"I would. And furthermore, few things make me more nervous and even less robust than visiting my aunt Dodie in New Jersey."

"I see," said Mr. Norton, swallowing. "A question: Are you merely stating the condition of things today? Or is there something more? Is it the case, perhaps, that your aunt Dodie has invited you to have tea with her in Maplefield?"

"Norton, you know me well. Yes, you have it exactly." Mr. Jones smoothed a napkin. "Here's my idea. Aunt Dodie is sure to serve me tea in the backyard. The mosquitoes haven't been bad this year, I'm sure her marigolds are blooming. And she'll want to talk about the neighbors, which she can do more effectively if she can point out their houses."

Mr. Norton raised his eyebrows and inclined his round head.

"What if, while I'm having tea with Aunt Dodie in the backyard, you took a bath upstairs in her bathroom?"

Mr. Norton bit another cracker.

"I don't know which window, when seen from the backyard, is the bathroom window exactly, but I know it's one of them. And I could just look at the back of the house. Knowing that you were in there having a soak would make all the difference."

Mr. Norton used his napkin to brush off the crumbs gathered on the bottom of his mustache, and then swept these from the table into the palm of his hand.

"How would you get me in? You know your aunt Dodie doesn't like me."

"I know. We'll have to sneak you in somehow. I suggest you hide in the bushes next to the front of the house. Then when Aunt Dodie is making the tea, I'll let you in and you can shoot up the front stairs."

"Yes, that could work," said Mr. Norton.

A week later they arrived at Aunt Dodie's house at the appointed hour. There had been some concern as to the possibility that Aunt Dodie might be waiting at the picture window, monitoring the sidewalk, so Mr. Jones had approached first alone, walking up the short front walk. Though he had not seen her at the window, still he waited at the door for a minute before motioning to Mr. Norton to join him—that is, to join him not on the doorstep but next to the doorstep in the bushes.

Mr. Jones rang the bell.

After a bit of shuffling from within, the door was opened and Aunt Dodie's small grizzled head appeared behind the storm door, which she opened a crack.

"Quick, come in," she said. "I don't like to stand at the door. For all I know there might be a strange man in the bushes."

Mr. Jones very nearly replied, "And what a man he is!"— which goes to show you that Mr. Jones's robustness had been boosted to nearly dangerous levels by the nights of good rest. Mr. Jones's natural prudence prevailed and he said, "You're so right, Aunt Dodie."

"I don't know if I'm right or wrong. I only know what I feel." Aunt Dodie raised her chin and cocked her cheek.

For a dreadful moment, Mr. Jones was unable to move, having no idea whether his aunt Dodie was demonstrating that she defied the world or was proffering her cheek to be kissed by her nephew.

Perhaps it was both.

At any rate, the dreadful moment passed, and Mr. Jones kissed her cheek.

"I thought we'd have our tea in the backyard," said Aunt Dodie, turning away. "I only need to assemble the things in the kitchen."

"Terrific," said Mr. Jones. "I'll be with you in a snap. I just need to tie my shoelace. Or something." Watching the old lady until she was safely in the kitchen, Mr. Jones stepped silently to the front door.

"Quick!" he whispered to the bushes.

Mr. Norton emerged, wiping the clinging brown fitzer branchlets from his sport coat with one hand, holding his bath brush, oatmeal soap, and towel in the other.

"The bathroom is the second door on the left," said Mr. Jones, as Mr. Norton swept gracefully up the stairs. Mr. Jones's robustness ticked slightly higher watching Mr. Norton. Though his physique was more farmer than ballet master, Mr. Norton moved with great poise.

"This is marvelous," said Mr. Jones, setting down the tea tray on the enameled table in the backyard under the little maple.

Aunt Dodie seated herself, with Mr. Jones's help, arranged

her utensils to her liking as Mr. Jones himself sat down, and said, "I'm glad to see living in New York City hasn't completely spoiled you."

"Thank you, Aunt Dodie."

"You aren't entirely ruined."

"I hope not, Aunt Dodie."

"You may make something of yourself yet."

"I'm almost sure of it, Aunt Dodie."

There was silence then, apart from the tweet of a suburban bird and a distant siren.

Aunt Dodie opened her mouth to say one thing, but then her head shot to the left and she said another. "What's that? What's that? Do you hear water running?"

"Water?"

"Water! Water running! And it's coming from my house!" And Aunt Dodie slapped the metal table.

Mr. Jones's mind raced. His aunt's suspicion rattled him to such an extent that he had a terrible urge to confess all. He nearly blurted out that there was now no longer a strange man in her bushes but one in her bathroom.

Instead of this thought, Mr. Jones glanced at the back of the house, and remembered Mr. Norton's bath brush, oatmeal soap, and towel, and he said, "Why, Aunt Dodie, I believe I saw your neighbor watering his lawn just now, and a lot of water it was."

"Oh?"

"I'm sure that's it."

"There, it's gone." Aunt Dodie sniffed.

Mr. Jones began relating the first of a couple of prepared stories about his cousin Jimmy—on his father's side, no relation to Aunt Dodie, making it all right—which she thoroughly enjoyed. Mr. Jones continued to run the conversation, buoyed by regular glances to the back of the house, reassured that, somewhere within, Mr. Norton was scrubbing his knees.

Occasionally, Aunt Dodie tried to take control of the conversation with a "But I thought you," and a couple of "Well, perhaps I'm too old to understand, but"s. Still Mr. Jones remained firmly in charge until he placed his teacup down softly in its saucer, then both cup and saucer on the table, and stood, saying, "Excuse me, I need to go to the loo."

Mr. Jones felt tremendously well as he strode away. Even his aunt Dodie's muttered "Always did have a weak bladder" couldn't dampen his feelings.

He pushed his head in at the bathroom door. Mr. Norton's musical voice was softly intoning:

O for a beaker full of the warm South,
Full of the true, the blushful Hippocrene...

"How's it going?" said Mr. Norton, putting down the bath brush.

"Couldn't be better. But I think I'd like to go now. I don't want to push my luck."

"Right you are. I shall rinse, dry, dress, and meet you at the bus stop in fifteen minutes."

"Thank you, Norton."

Returned to the backyard, Mr. Jones sat down, heaving a great sigh. "This is the life!" he said. "Look at everything you have." He waved his hands a bit. "Marigolds, fascinating neighbors, and hardly a mosquito." He shooed one of the few from the sugar bowl. "I wish I didn't have to leave."

As Mr. Jones brought in the things from the backyard and helped Aunt Dodie in loading the dishwasher, she seemed distracted—disappointed even—perhaps feeling cheated by the disappearance of the nervous nephew she had anticipated.

"What's gotten into you anyway?" she said, at last. "You're different."

"Am I?" said Mr. Jones with a giggle. "Well, different or not, I must be going."

Standing at the front door, Aunt Dodie was this time unmistakable in her movements: She only stuck out her chin.

On the bus ride back to Manhattan, Mr. Jones was nearly giddy, his glee at having bested his formidable aunt practically raising him off his seat. "And how was your bath?" he said at last.

"It was very fine," said Mr. Norton, turning from his examination of the New Jersey landscape. "I had a little trouble with the hot-water control at first, but that was soon sorted. I admired your aunt Dodie's bath salts. Didn't take any! No, sir. But I admired them."

"You let me know the brand names," said Mr. Jones, tapping Mr. Norton's thigh. "I'll get you ten bottles."

Their New Jersey high emboldened them to tackle other challenges.

A dentist appointment had been a bit of a stumper at first. After days of fret and worry, it was Mr. Norton who remembered that his old college maintained a health club that stood just down the block and across the street from the dentist's office. He would inquire as to its bathing facilities.

It had them. And, more important, it boasted a hot-water pool. And so, by keeping one eye open, and as long as the dental hygienist wasn't standing in the way of the window, Mr. Jones could just see the top of the building where Mr. Norton sat serenely in hot water. That and the novocaine had gotten Mr. Jones through.

Seasons passed. Aunt Dodie invited Mr. Jones to a Memorial

Day picnic, a Columbus Day brunch, and a Christmas Day dinner and all had gone well, Mr. Jones assuring her that the sound of rushing water she seemed always to hear was merely the onset of mild tinnitus.

But then, in the spring, came a crisis that defied Mr. Jones and Mr. Norton to find a solution. Mr. Jones had reached that particular age when not only Insomnia crept up on one unawares but also old college classmates. They suddenly seemed to feel that what's life all about really if not to revisit old pals? Hey, weren't those the grandest days of our lives and shouldn't we relive them, etc.? Mr. Jones wasn't so sure. Nevertheless, there was no getting around it, he had been invited to a reunion of the second tenor section of his college men's chorus. Mr. Jones was assured that it would not be the same without him. The gathering was to take place in the Scheherazade Room at the Melford Hotel in midtown.

It was an appalling idea, thought Mr. Jones. Unfortunately, straightforward refusal was something he had never gotten the hang of. The roundabout half-truths and evasions that Mr. Jones replied with were ignored. Like a man caught in an evil tunnel of fate, Mr. Jones saw no way out and agreed to meet the men with whom, thirty years ago, he had warbled the second treble line.

"What can we do?" said Mr. Jones. "Can we knock on hotel doors and ask if you can use the bathroom for an hour? I don't think so."

"It would be awkward," said Mr. Norton. "Perhaps we could book a room for the day? I'll phone the hotel." Rising, he walked to the hall. When he returned, Mr. Jones could see the news was bad.

"The hotel's booked solid until the summer."

Mr. Norton sat down and Mr. Jones poured him another cup of tea. They stirred their tea gloomily.

"I've an idea," said Mr. Norton. "Why must it be a bath I'm sitting in? What's to say it couldn't be a bath sitting in me?"

Mr. Jones stopped stirring.

"What I mean is, do you see that teapot there, in front of us on the table, and this teacup? Of course you do, you're not blind. What if I put this hot tea in me from that pot, and you just kept an eye on that pot? We'll still be connected by the hot water. When you have dinner with those nice gentlemen, you just order a pot—mind that you order a pot, not a cup—and I'll order the same, elsewhere in the hotel. We'll each have a pot of tea in front of us. Different pots, of course. But they will be united by their pottiness. So anytime you feel unsure or panicky, you just get an eyeful of that teapot, and then you might as well be getting an eyeful of me because I'll be drinking tea at that very moment and you'll know it!" Mr. Norton smiled through his mustache encouragingly.

"Hmm," said Mr. Jones. "Stare at the teapot?" He stared at their own teapot, which was colored a sap green with a stripe of coral pink around the lid. "It doesn't sound quite as effective as you sitting in a hot bath. Will it be as strong, though, I wonder? Let's give it a test."

Mr. Jones tapped a finger to his nose.

"Norton, please take your tea to your room right now and shut the door hard." Mr. Norton took his tea, his paper, and two crackers to his room and pulled the door tightly shut.

Mr. Jones waited for the inevitable feeling of unease to arrive—the simple shutting of Mr. Norton's door was enough to make Mr. Jones wonder what he had done wrong. He began to sweat gently. His teeth tingled. The skin on the backs of his hands began to tighten and one pinkie twitched.

And then Mr. Jones gazed at the teapot and imagined its warm contents sloshing around inside Mr. Norton's tublike belly. He was a farmer! Round! A comforting water tower.

His thoughts acted like a genie, like a witch's spell, like a pixie's charm, and the fear was driven away.

"Norty!" he said. "It worked!"

Mr. Norton swiftly opened the door, which showed that he had been standing immediately behind it. Anxious about the results, no doubt.

"Just make sure you ask for a teapot," he said, beaming, "a nice round one."

On the day of the reunion, Mr. Jones arrived early in the private room and immediately asked for a pot of tea from the very nice attendant. And by the time the sentimental gathering was concluded, which would have reduced Mr. Jones to a quivering jelly unaided, it had been three pots of tea to Mr. Jones, which also left him quivering, but not a jelly and not unhappy.

In the dining room on the first floor of the hotel, Mr. Norton too had his pot of tea, along with a steak frites and the paper.

The teapot scheme soon worked so well that Mr. Norton no longer took a bath each night but fixed himself a pot of tea instead. It was not long before Mr. Jones never left the apartment without one of their small teapots bundled up in his bag.

Years later on a winter night, as the freezing rain lashed their living-room window, Mr. Jones and Mr. Norton again sat at the table with their tea. Mr. Norton snorted from time to time from behind the sports section. Mr. Jones laid out a game of solitaire, one of the large two-pack games he liked.

Placing a black ten–red nine–black eight combination on a red jack, he said, "Norty, what will I do if you're ever no longer here?"

Mr. Norton looked around the paper. "Oh, pooh," he said.

"No, I'm serious. What if it proves to be true that I can't live without you?"

Mr. Norton put the paper down. "Nonsense!"

"But where will I find the strength to go on without you?"

"There will always be hot water snug in its caul. In this case, tea."

Mr. Jones and Mr. Norton lifted their fine china cups to each other, the ones with the little birds painted on them in blue and white, and drank.

THE DOORMAN'S REPOSE

MR. BUNCHLEY sat at a small table at the back of a long, narrow tavern. The Doorman's Repose was where building attendants of all kinds liked to take their ease after hours. It was the end of a hot summer day. A glass of Chardonnay and a plate of English crackers stood in front of Mr. Bunchley. Trying without success to bend his concentration to the book—about the care of zinnias—that lay open on the table next to the crackers, Mr. Bunchley was distracted by the loud discussion going on at the bar.

"I tell you," said a man in a gray uniform with pale yellow stripes, "this is a city of a hundred, no, a thousand, no, make it ten thousand separate and completely disconnected circles of people. They're like tops all spinning. But nobody ever touches nobody else. Everybody lives in their own tiny world with other people just like themselves."

"You said it," said the man's neighbor, whose uniform was blue and featured gold epaulettes.

"Nobody knows nobody else. Everybody in their own little world. You're here. I'm there. He's over there. We may live in the same building, but it's like we're on different planets!"

"You said it!" And the fringes on the gold epaulettes bounced a little up and down.

Not wanting to stay silent anymore, Mr. Bunchley closed his book and tucked it under his arm. Lifting his glass, plate, and himself from his spot at the table, he moved to the bar.

"Excuse me," said Mr. Bunchley, "you didn't say it."

"What do you mean, I didn't say it?" said the one in gray.

"At least, what you said had no basis in fact," said Mr. Bunchley. He arranged himself on a stool.

"What do you mean?" said the one in blue.

"Yeah, what do you mean?" said the one in gray.

"I mean simply this. This city is more interconnected than the loops of yarn in your grandmother's sweater. Pull on one thread, undo one loop, and the whole thing unravels. Each loop loops around the one above, is held by the loops to left and right, and is itself looped around by the one below. The only things fixed are the knots at the first and the last. So it is with our city. I can think of a hundred instances. The story of Mrs. Sleeplater's glasses comes to mind. It was like this—"

"Here!" said the one in gray. "If you're going to tell one of your stories, I need a pint." He motioned to the barman.

"What I mean," said Mr. Bunchley, pausing for a moment to have a sip of his wine, "is that we are all of us, as a people, interconnected."

"No, we aren't."

"Here's what I mean," continued Mr. Bunchley. "You, Mr. Macadam," he said, addressing the one in gray, "and you, Mr. Wissel," addressing the one in blue, "and I, as doormen, are notably connected to all walks of life, high and low, weak and strong, rich and poor, young and old. From the Wall Street banker, to the garbage collector. From the lady in the penthouse, to the hobo on the corner bench. We doormen are not unlike the hub of a great wheel. The connecting spokes run from us out to the rim in all directions."

"Yeah, sure," said Mr. Macadam, "but that still don't mean nothing. We're the hub, like you said, the axle."

"Yes, Mr. Macadam, but I prefer hub," said Mr. Bunchley. He put down his glass.

"Hub, then," said Mr. Macadam. "Let me finish. Sure, we're at the center. Sure, we know everything and everybody."

"And keep the whole thing turning," said Mr. Wissel, smiling at his cleverness. "Couldn't turn without us."

"Right," said Mr. Macadam, "but that still don't mean everybody else ain't disconnected. Disconnected. Dis is what I'm saying."

"Ah, but don't you see?" said Mr. Bunchley. "The wheel only turns because the rim is itself connected." Mr. Bunchley bit vigorously into a cracker.

He chewed for a bit and then said, "I propose a wager. A bet. If I can show you that twelve city residents, from twelve separate circles, as you call them, have made a connection with each other, one after the other, in twelve hours, will you buy me a cup of tea?"

"And if you don't?" said Mr. Macadam.

"I'll buy you both one of those brown beverages you're consuming so heartily."

"Done," said Mr. Macadam. "But how are you going to do it?"

"Well, first let's agree on what having a connection means. I propose a definition. A connection is made when at least one party would feel the lack of the other."

"Huh?" said Mr. Macadam.

"I mean, two or more individuals are connected when they have an effect on each other. It's simple. Look. You and I and Mr. Wissel are connected."

"Sure, but we know each other."

"Yes, of course. And if we didn't know each other, our lives would be different. Am I right?"

"Why, I guess that's so," said Mr. Wissel.

"I would miss you if you left," said Mr. Bunchley. "My life would be different if I hadn't met you. If not for our connection, Mr. Macadam, I would never know when the Super Bowl takes place and as a result would wonder where everyone was. Why the lobby was so deserted."

Mr. Macadam frowned but nodded.

"And if I wasn't connected to you, Mr. Wissel, I would never have learned of the hatter on Fifth Avenue, who has ever since I entered his establishment served me so well. Without our connection, my hats would be demonstrably shabbier. You see? And I am always most grateful for this, by the way. Thank you, again, Mr. Wissel."

"You are most welcome," said Mr. Wissel.

"The definition, for our purposes then, is that a connection exists when its absence would be felt. All right?"

"All right," said Mr. Macadam.

"Fine. Agreed. Let me begin."

"Hold it," said Mr. Macadam. He took a long draft of his beer, replaced the glass on the coaster, then wiped his mouth with a white handkerchief. "Connections, effects, feelings, fine. Whatever. But how do we know? Who's going to referee this? Who's going to establish the facts? The real jam, the honest to Pete of the situation. How will we know you aren't making it all up?"

"I suggest that Mr. Wissel be the referee. He has been a doorman for twenty-two years. He knows a great deal. I just mentioned his knowledge of hatters. I leave it to Mr. Wissel to judge my story. Fair enough?"

Mr. Wissel sat a little straighter and raised his bushy eyebrows at Mr. Macadam.

"Fair enough, then," said Mr. Macadam, "if it'll make you happy. But I'll be listening closely for any baloney."

"There will be no baloney. There will be twelve people, twelve connections, in twelve hours," said Mr. Bunchley.

Mr. Bunchley adjusted his plumpish thighs on the barstool. "I believe it was Mr. E. M. Forster who said, 'Only connect.' Was it not? And as Mr. Forster would be the first person, I think, to agree that a connection can only be shown through a properly told story—I stress *properly told*—some of the details of what I have to say, the *dialogue* and so forth, might be, let's say, made up by myself. But *only*, I stress, in service to the truth of the story. Mr. Wissel, you are a well-read man. You have read your Dickens. You have read your *New York Times* Sunday edition. You know what is true and what is not. Again, I turn to you to referee."

Mr. Macadam crossed his arms and gave Mr. Wissel a sour look, but said nothing.

We will begin the contest at a quarter to nine in the morning (said Mr. Bunchley) for at precisely that time yesterday, Mrs. J. G. Sleeplater concludes that she has lost her glasses and that she will never find them again.

The evening before, in fact, she was sketching out this hypothesis on a provisional basis. She said to me, "Mr. Bunchley, have you perchance seen my glasses? I can't find them anywhere. I am beginning to think that they are gone for good."

I responded in the negative—naturally, by the way, any

connections between me and the subjects of this story do not count in our tally.

("Naturally," said Mr. Macadam.)

Back to yesterday morning. "My glasses, they're gone!" Mrs. J. G. Sleeplater wails. It is now roughly ten minutes to nine. At this point she is wailing so loudly that she attracts the attention of Alehandro, the man standing on the scaffold eighteen floors up and just outside Mrs. J. G. Sleeplater's window.

Alehandro is a good-hearted young man from Costa Rica— he once commented on the beauty of my carnations. *Espléndido*, was, I think, his exact remark. Now, even though he is standing on a platform wobbling hundreds of feet in the air, a situation that in most people would focus the attention strictly on personal survival, Alehandro, seeing another person in difficulties, wants to help.

"*Señora, señora*," he says.

"Who's that?" says Mrs. J. G. Sleeplater, and she goes to the window.

"It is I, Alehandro, repairing your crumbling masonry."

"Never mind my masonry," she says, and she slides open the window a little. "How can I help you? Do you need to use the loo? Like a glass of water? Run out of sunscreen?"

"It is I who can help you, *señora*!" says Alehandro. "Your glasses, they are here behind the green vase on the dresser. I can see them because they are in between the green vase and the window. I can see them from out here. You can't see them from in there. You see, *señora*?"

Mrs. J. G. Sleeplater goes to the dresser, shifts the green vase, and shouts, "Eureka! My glasses!"

She places them on her nose and, peering through them, looks closely at the young man who has helped her.

"What did you say your name was?" she says.

"Alehandro, *señora*," he says.

"Thank you, Alehandro. These glasses are essential. I'll need them tonight when I give my weekly knitting lesson to Victoria."

"*Muy bien, señora*," says Alehandro.

("That's one connection between two separate circles. Are we agreed, Mr. Wissel?"

"Perfectly agreed, Mr. Bunchley.")

A short time later, Alehandro unhooks his safety harness from the scaffolding railing and climbs over the parapet, having raised the platform to the roof. He takes the long slow ride down in Elevator Number Two. He's on his way to get his morning cup of coffee at the corner deli. He always goes to the U Like Deli.

Yoshi, the granddaughter of the owner, makes the café con leche the way Alehandro likes it and already has one ready for him when he gets there.

"*Cómo estás?*" she says.

"I'll tell you a thing," he says. "If I ever build a house, it will be one story high. Not two. Not three. Just one. And even that story will be short."

"Poor Alehandro," says Yoshi, and she hands him his drink. "Take a break. Drink coffee. Feel better. And now you'll have to excuse me because I have to take a delivery to Mr. Sherman."

("That's two," said Mr. Wissel.

"What time are we at?" said Mr. Macadam.

"Approximately a quarter after eleven," said Mr. Bunchley.

"That means you got nine and a half hours to do ten more," said Mr. Macadam with a confident smile.

"Okay," said Mr. Bunchley.)

Yoshi walks the few steps to 777 Garden Avenue carrying a

yellow plastic bag printed with the U Like Deli logo, a large U and a smaller LIKE in bold blue letters. The bag contains three tins of Spam, one can of condensed milk, one big box of Lipton tea, and a banana.

("I'll tell you how I know what was in the bag," said Mr. Bunchley. "Yoshi always tells me when Mr. Sherman has asked for anything unusual. Two extra tins of Spam. Frankly, that's not good. It indicates to me, his doorman, that he, Mr. Sherman, is once again convinced that there will be some kind of end-of-the-world event soon. Anyway, I mustn't wander from my story.")

Mr. Sherman opens his door to Yoshi and says, "Ah, the Spam. Good to have Spam. Put it anywhere."

Yoshi puts the bag on Mr. Sherman's kitchen counter and says, "Is there anything special for tomorrow?"

"I think I'll up the Spam order. Make it four tins of Spam. I don't like what's happening in Australia. Bad signs in Sydney. Malfeasance in Melbourne. Perils in Perth. The island continent could go up any minute in a great big blue ball of fire and ashes. But when it does, I'll be ready. I've got enough Spam to last me a year."

"That's good, Mr. Sherman."

"All right, Yoshi. Same time tomorrow."

Yoshi departs. She glances at the kitchen clock. It's ten minutes before noon.

("Three. Agreed?" said Mr. Bunchley.

"Agreed," said Mr. Wissel.)

One hour later, the alarm goes off in the kitchen and Mr. Sherman sits up like a snapping turtle.

"Wha? Are we under attack?" He looks around a bit and then remembers he's set the alarm to remind him of the laundry in the basement. "Ah. The laundry's done. The sheets must be dry."

Mr. Sherman takes the elevator to the basement.

There he meets Agnes, who hands Mr. Sherman his blue laundry basket, filled with neatly folded, polka-dotted sheets.

Agnes works for a number of our residents. She was raised in Jamaica. "I can't abide this cold weather, Mr. Bunchley," she often says to me, even in the spring or fall. "But with the Lord's help, I will." That's Agnes.

"I needed the dryer for Miss Nancy," says Agnes, "so I folded your sheets, Mr. Sherman, which were done and all, so I did take them out for the reason to put Miss Nancy's wash in. But I folded yours there."

"Your name is Agnes, and you work for Nancy. Is that right?"

"That's right, Mr. Sherman."

("You're telling me folding someone's clothes for them is a connection?" said Mr. Macadam.

"That's exactly what I'm telling you," said Mr. Bunchley.

"How do we know she didn't stick a wad a' gum in them?"

"Even had she done so, it's still a connection." Mr. Bunchley looked at Mr. Wissel.

"Four," said Mr. Wissel, making a note on the back of a napkin.)

The time is now one fifteen.

Agnes and Mr. Sherman ride the elevator up together, Mr. Sherman getting off at the eighth floor, and Agnes getting off at the eleventh floor.

"Miss Nancy, your sheets and towels will be done in an hour and in the meantime I will be busying myself seeing to the kitchen," she says to Miss Nancy.

"Oh, thank you, dear," says Miss Nancy.

Nancy Clover is a tall woman with large eyes and a face like a sheepdog. This is odd, because she is devoted to her cat. She is a publicist for several aging actors.

"Mr. Sherman was looking pleased as punch. I saw him just now," says Agnes.

"He must be thinking about the end of the world again. He does take a great deal of comfort in that idea," says Miss Nancy.

"But the world is keeping on going. Sure enough it is," says Agnes.

"Yes. That is worrisome for him. Still, let's look on the bright side. The world will end one day. Boy, I sure would like to get that job. Publicizing the end of the world. That could be huge!"

"Lordy, Miss Nancy!"

"Come on, Carole Lombard, time for walkies," says Miss Nancy to her cat.

Miss Nancy, apart from being a tall woman with the face and saliva of a Saint Bernard, or did I mean sheepdog, either way, doesn't matter, is the only member of my building who walks her cat, Carole Lombard. Whether Carole Lombard likes to be walked on a leash is not known for sure, maybe not even by Carole Lombard. Sometimes she runs ahead, pulling Miss Nancy; sometimes she hangs behind, being dragged by Miss Nancy. Either way, there seems to be a lot of tension in that leash, which brings me to my next point. Is this not a perfect, even a literal example of a connection across social circles? It's even across mammalian circles, primate to carnivore, or human to cat.

("What?" said Mr. Macadam. "You propose to use a house pet as one of your connections?"

"I do," said Mr. Bunchley. "Mr. Wissel? Can I have a ruling?"

"Human to cat as an example of a connection across social circles, eh? Well, I believe I must accept it based on the International Standards of Companionship as established, if I remember correctly, in Uppsala, Sweden, in 1979," said Mr. Wissel.

"Oh, for Pete's sake!" said Mr. Macadam.

"Five for Agnes and Miss Nancy. Six for Miss Nancy and the cat," said Mr. Wissel.)

At two twenty, forty yards down Seventy-seventh Street, Carole Lombard falls into conversation with a piebald pigeon. I can't be sure of all the details, but from my vantage point the conversation looked quite a lot like this:

Carole Lombard starts: "Hey, you!"

"Who?" says the pigeon.

"You."

"You mean, me?"

"You."

"What about it?"

"You."

"Oh, yeah?"

"Yeah."

(Mr. Bunchley raised his eyebrow at Mr. Wissel.

"Cat to pigeon?" said Mr. Wissel. "Well, I guess if I'm going to accept cats I'm going to have to accept pigeons. But it's not like the cat and the pigeon as you describe them are close."

"Exactly!" said Mr. Macadam, slapping the bar. "Carole Lombard and the pigeon is the opposite of a connection. That's a disconnection! You've got to subtract one."

Mr. Bunchley pursed his lips. "I take your point."

"Ha!"

"But I don't concede the point. By our definition, a connection exists where the lack thereof produces a noticeable result. What is the noticeable result if Carole Lombard and the pigeon are not connected? A moribund state in each. A listless cat. A pigeon who lacks sparkle."

"Bthzthzthzthzthzthzthz!" said Mr. Macadam, producing a Bronx cheer.

"Look at us!" said Mr. Bunchley. "Take us as another example! We are at odds. But...we need each other. Without anyone pushing against us, we fall over. Have you, a lifelong New Yorker, ever been to Los Angeles? There is no one to lean on there. No one's pushing. It's all friendliness. You fall over."

Mr. Macadam was silent.

"If I may use another example. The Hell Gate Bridge firmly and proudly upholds each train going to and coming from Boston because some beams push and some beams pull. It's like this—"

"All right, all right," said Mr. Macadam.

"Seven," said Mr. Wissel.)

Shortly after his conversation with Carole Lombard, the pigeon flies to a windowsill on the seventh floor where he knows a few bread crumbs are waiting for him. The pigeon perches a bit. He fluffs his feathers as he thinks about the things he said to Carole and Carole said to him. He coos quietly in a distraught manner.

When Fred opens the window and passes out a few more crumbs, the pigeon just steps to one side and eyes Fred with his head cocked. Fred turns his grizzled face and long nose to the pigeon. The pigeon nods and blinks once very slowly.

("You're making this up!" said Mr. Macadam. "Besides, how do we know Fred fed exactly *that* pigeon?"

Mr. Bunchley looked at Mr. Wissel.

"Eight," said Mr. Wissel.)

At this point, Fred takes a long nap.

When he wakes, he fixes himself some tea with biscuits. And the upshot is, I'm sorry to say, he doesn't come out of his room on the seventh floor until seven forty-five in the evening.

("Aha!" said Mr. Macadam. "You've got exactly one hour to make four more connections—and they'd better all be human!" Mr. Macadam beetled his eyebrows at Mr. Bunchley.

Mr. Bunchley calmly resumed his story.)

Fred puts on his best white shirt and buttons it to the top. He slips into his best khaki trousers and tucks the shirttails somewhat carelessly. Then, with only slippers on his feet, he rides Elevator Number Three to the third floor and walks down the hallway there to apartment 31, where he presses the bell.

Delmore Bishop, our poet, opens the door. He smiles and, without saying a word, leads Fred to the small table in the apartment's one room where a chessboard stands. Every Tuesday evening, and this was a Tuesday, it is their habit to play chess. Now, I don't know to an absolute surety whether or not any words are spoken at all between Fred and Delmore Bishop, but I do know that Fred wins three games out of five.

("Nine," said Mr. Wissel.

"Playing chess is a connection I suppose," said Mr. Macadam.

"Of course, it is," said Mr. Bunchley.

"Oh, I know, the Uppsala Convention." Mr. Macadam scowled. "Wait a second. How long did they play chess?"

"Approximately two hours," said Mr. Bunchley.

"Then I win!" Mr. Macadam thumped the bar and took a swallow of beer. "Two hours puts the time at nine forty-five, at least. And you're still missing three connections!"

"I do not quite concede defeat yet, Mr. Macadam, because at sixteen minutes after eight our super, Oskar, arrives at Mr. Bishop's apartment to fix the squeak in the door. He says 'Good evening,' 'Who's winning?,' and 'Is that the famous La Paz opening I see?' Also, he fixes the squeak."

"Ten," said Mr. Wissel.)

Eleven minutes later, at eight twenty-seven, Miss Victoria appears at Oskar's office door to ask to borrow a number seven Allen wrench, which she needs to tune her accordion. Lucky for Victoria, Oskar had returned to his office two minutes earlier. Oskar opens the door, and Victoria asks for the wrench. Then Victoria offers Oskar a plate of chocolate chip cookies that she baked that afternoon. Victoria's visit to Oskar takes eight minutes.

("Eleven," said Mr. Wissel.

"By my calculation, you've got ten minutes," said Mr. Macadam.)

Miss Victoria steps into Elevator Number Two in the basement at eight thirty-seven exactly. If all goes smoothly the next stop will take her to Mrs. Sleeplater's apartment on the eighteenth floor. Miss Victoria has a weekly knitting lesson there, which she squeezes in between her accordion lesson with Mr. Bellows, who comes to her apartment at seven thirty, and her bedtime at ten.

The travel time from the basement to floor eighteen is, if uninterrupted, one minute and fifty seconds, a time that would put Miss Victoria face-to-face with Mrs. Sleeplater at just before eight thirty-nine.

However, elevator trips with no stops are rare. The elevator stops at the lobby, where Mr. Pearl (the high-school principal), Mr. Fanshaw (the TV news producer), and Mrs. Zeebruggen get on.

No one speaks.

("Aha!" said Mr. Macadam. "No one speaks. No connections!" Rubbing his hands together, he gave Mr. Wissel a threatening look.)

There was some smiling and nodding at one another, but— as you say, Mr. Macadam—there are no real connections.

The elevator door begins to close at eight thirty-eight and

then rolls open again at eight thirty-eight and ten seconds when an umbrella is jammed into the narrowing sliver of space made by the closing door.

Mrs. MacDougal steps in.

The elevator begins to ascend. A silence weighs on the riders. The presence of Mrs. MacDougal squashes any chance of conversation as everyone in the building, in general, and in this elevator, in particular, is vaguely afraid of her. Mr. Fanshaw and Mr. Pearl look straight ahead. Mrs. Zeebruggen rummages in her bag noisily with one hand. Miss Victoria looks at the powdered underside of Mrs. MacDougal's chin.

The elevator slows, clicks a bit, shudders, comes to a stop, and opens its door at floor five. Mr. Pearl wishes everyone good night and steps off.

Mrs. MacDougal jabs at the Door Close button, and after five seconds of delay, the elevator door closes.

They continue up. The small round window in the door, like a porthole, allows in a brief ray of light as they pass each floor.

At floor twelve, Mrs. Zeebruggen and Mr. Fanshaw depart without saying anything.

It is now eight forty-two.

Twenty seconds later, Mrs. MacDougal steps off at floor fifteen. But instead of proceeding down the hall, she turns to face Victoria.

Holding the door open with her left hand, Mrs. MacDougal says, "Is it you whom I hear playing the accordion?" and she booms out the "whom" like a horn.

Miss Victoria's eyes grow bigger, but she doesn't say anything.

"It is not a ladylike instrument and I recommend strongly, strongly, that you give up this unbecoming habit. In fact," she lets go of the door, "I think I'll bring it up at the next board meeting. I plan to make 777 Garden Avenue an accordion-free building. Good night!"

Victoria, gulping, presses Door Close as hard as she can (without punching).

The time is eight forty-three.

Elevator Number Two covers the last three floors in record time—fifteen seconds.

Mrs. Sleeplater opens the door to Victoria's ring and welcomes her in as she leads the way to the living room.

She says, placing her glasses on her nose, "Have you got your little masterpiece?"

Victoria pulls a small half sock on four needles out of her knitting bag. She says, "The ankle's all done."

"Wonderful," says Mrs. Sleeplater. "Tonight we will tackle the tricky German heel. After we first have some chamomile tea, that is."

"Goody," says Victoria.

And at that moment, the wall clock in Mrs. Sleeplater's living room chimes brightly three times indicating the three-quarter hour.

Mr. Wissel checked the back of his napkin. Mr. Macadam sat breathing deeply. Mr. Bunchley placed a cracker into his mouth and chewed demurely.

Mr. Wissel said, "Are we not counting Victoria to Mrs. MacDougal because Victoria didn't say anything?"

"That is correct," said Mr. Bunchley.

"Okay, then," Mr. Wissel continued. "Then that's Mrs. J.G. Sleeplater of the eighteenth floor, to Alehandro of the swaying platform on the outside of the eighteenth floor, to Yoshi at the U Like Deli, to Mr. Sherman of apartment 8D, to Agnes from Jamaica, to Miss Nancy on floor eleven, to Carole Lombard the cat, to a pigeon, to Fred on the seventh floor, to Delmore Bishop the poet, to Oskar the super, to Miss Victoria the knitting student, back up to Mrs. J. G. Sleepwater on the eighteenth floor. That's twelve all right. Twelve residents. Twelve connections. Twelve hours."

Apart from some heavy sipping, there was silence at the bar of the Doorman's Repose.

At last, Mr. Bunchley said, "I'll have that cup of tea now, Mr. Macadam."

CHRIS RASCHKA has made more than sixty books for children, including *Yo! Yes?*, *Five for a Little One*, *A Ball for Daisy*, and, with Vladimir Radunsky, *Alphabetabum*, which is published by The New York Review Children's Collection. His work has earned one Caldecott Honor and two Caldecott Medals, as well as the Ezra Jack Keats Award, and his books have been selected five times for *The New York Times* Best Illustrated Books list. He lives in New York City.

MUNRO LEAF AND ROBERT LAWSON
Wee Gillis

RHODA LEVINE AND EVERETT AISON
Arthur

RHODA LEVINE AND EDWARD GOREY
He Was There from the Day We Moved In
Three Ladies Beside the Sea

RHODA LEVINE AND KARLA KUSKIN
Harrison Loved His Umbrella

BETTY JEAN LIFTON AND EIKOH HOSOE
Taka-chan and I

ASTRID LINDGREN
Mio, My Son
Seacrow Island

NORMAN LINDSAY
The Magic Pudding

ERIC LINKLATER
The Wind on the Moon

J. P. MARTIN
Uncle
Uncle Cleans Up

JOHN MASEFIELD
The Box of Delights
The Midnight Folk

WILLIAM McCLEERY AND WARREN CHAPPELL
Wolf Story

JEAN MERRILL AND RONNI SOLBERT
The Elephant Who Liked to Smash Small Cars
The Pushcart War

E. NESBIT
The House of Arden

ALFRED OLLIVANT'S
Bob, Son of Battle: The Last Gray Dog of Kenmuir
A New Version by LYDIA DAVIS

EUGENE OSTASHEVSKY, TRANSLATOR
The Fire Horse: Children's Poems
by Vladimir Mayakovsky, Osip Mandelstam, and Daniil Kharms

DANIEL PINKWATER
Lizard Music

OTFRIED PREUSSLER
Krabat & the Sorcerer's Mill
The Little Water Sprite
The Little Witch
The Robber Hotzenplotz

VLADIMIR RADUNSKY AND CHRIS RASCHKA
Alphabetabum

ALASTAIR REID AND BOB GILL
Supposing . . .

ALASTAIR REID AND BEN SHAHN
Ounce Dice Trice

BARBARA SLEIGH
Carbonel and Calidor
Carbonel: The King of the Cats
The Kingdom of Carbonel

E. C. SPYKMAN
Terrible, Horrible Edie

ANNA STAROBINETS
Catlantis

CATHERINE STORR
The Complete Polly and the Wolf

FRANK TASHLIN
The Bear That Wasn't

VAL TEAL AND ROBERT LAWSON
The Little Woman Wanted Noise